The Telling Of
My
Marching Band Story

by

Will Todd

CreateSpace Edition

Table of Contents

Prologue

I gotta tell you... actually, I don't "got" to I suppose; for one thing, there's nothing really forcing me to sit down and write this, not even any oh-my-god-I-just-*gotta*-tell-this-story sort of thing; for another thing, I probably shouldn't have used "gotta" like that instead of "got to" even though that's more like what I talk like, and you gotta decide how you're gonna write, like you talk or like something else, like maybe a compromise for easier readability in which case I probably should've just used the grammatically more correct "have to" though – to tell The Truth – it's really more of a "want".

So.

I *want* to tell you (actually "wanna", but I'm gonna-- going to compromise) this is the trickiest part you're going to have to deal with. *Dangit* - except you're not supposed to end a sentence with "with". For some reason I've never really understood, it's bad to end a sentence with "with", a "preposition" ("before the position"), another grammatical thing, like words like "with" and "to" and... several others, though I couldn't tell you why. I think it's an east coast thing. But since this story is going to take place in the Midwest, maybe I can ignore it. Though you still want people on the east coast to read your stuff, so I don't know. It *is* a rule.

Though if a sentence is understandable, why not use it? Besides, you don't want your sentences to be just like everybody else's sentences, do you? It's the thoughts behind them that count, right?

This is gonna be harder than I thought.

You need a good first sentence. Everybody says so. Something to "lock" your audience in right away. (You'll understand just how clever that "lock" reference was when you get deeper into the story.) (If you remember it by then, which you probably won't.) (Okay, forget it.) Ideally, your first sentence should suck people in, keep them reading. About the worst way you could start a story is just to ramble. Which, I know, I know, an excellent example of which would be what I've been doing so far.

But.

My story hasn't really started yet. That's what "Prologue" means, "before the story". And the reason I wanted one was to explain before the story really starts about the two "I"s.

So.

When an author (I'm not real comfortable with that word "author") (for obvious reasons) (at least to me) (you'll see why) (think "parentheticals"); When a writer uses the word "I" in a novel (I'm not all that comfortable with the word "novel", either) (for not as obvious of reasons) (though there's some debate (or is going to be) as to if that's what this really is anyway) (a novel, I mean); When a writer uses the word "I" in a work (I'm not real thrilled with that either) (Okay, how 'bout this?): When a person uses the word "I" in a story, there's a couple of things.

There's the "I" that means whoever actually wrote the stuff is talking – I did this, I did that - in which case you assume what's being said is true or "non-fiction", as it's called. Then there's the "I" that means a *character* is talking, which is in the area of "fiction", or made-up stuff. The tricky part is that in fiction there can actually be two "I"s, too. The first always appears in quotes and indicates that some character is talking – "I did this (made-up thing), I did that (made-up thing)" – it's dialogue, really. But there's another possible "I" that doesn't go in quotes. It's not always used, but if it is, it means the story has a character called a *Narrator*, and everything is told from this one person's single P.O.V. Meaning "point of view". Which I guess I could've just used instead of the abbreviation. But you have to make decisions and a lot of times you're not sure which is better, even depending on how you figure your audience.

I'll just use "perspective" next time.

Maybe.

Probably.

I don't know, the problem is I tend to overanalyze. And every time you start a new sentence you have to pick out just what you wanna-- want to say. (And how to say it.) (And what *not* to say.) (Like that last parenthetical – I decided to put it in even though it was definitely iffy.) (That one, too.) (It can get out of hand.) It can get out of hand. So as a general rule, I've decided on something.

This.

The Truth.

I'm gonna let The Truth be my guide.

Well, as much as possible. I'm remembering most of this story, not making it up, and it was a while ago, so it's not going to be exact. Like those books where the person supposedly remembers entire conversations and whole honkin' blocks of things that people said years ago. No way. I can't remember exactly what I said five minutes ago, let alone five years ago. So just to let you know that I'm aware of that kind of stuff, and I'm going to try not to do any of it because it would bug me if I were you. And so for the most part, you can assume that most of what you are about to read is true. And where it isn't...

I'll let you know.

Now back to the "I". I need to decide which "I" to use. The first kind of "I" would be Me, the Storyteller, and would make this non-fiction. Which isn't entirely The Truth. The second kind of "I" would be a character being a Narrator and would make this fiction. Which isn't entirely The Truth, either.

Sooooo...

The heck with it, I'll use Third Person.

See, using any of those "I" approaches I talked about before is called telling a story in the First Person, which means telling everything from a single... perspective. But there's also something called Third Person, which means telling a story from a third party perspective; a – and this is key – *infallible* third party perspective. All-knowing. That's why it's also called using the "omnipotent" voice, like some god-like revealer who knows about everything and what everybody is doing and especially thinking *all the time*.

You know, the more I explain about this, the more I like it.

So!

Third Person it is.

Besides, it'll give me another take at a First Sentence...

Act One: Fresh Man

Scene 1: Orientation

Like most things worth telling, this one started out a little unusual.

Will was all by himself. This, alone, wouldn't have been all that unusual since Will spent a lot of time by himself, even liked it, except that he was all by himself right smack in the middle of one of the largest college campuses in the Midwest. True, it was still mid-summer-stasis, weeks before the start of fall semester and another school year, but where was everybody?

Normally, there'd be thousands of students in the general vicinity getting matriculated, maybe even educated, and hundreds in particular trafficking through this very spot, which was called The Diag because it's where two major campus walkways crisscrossed to form an "X" and because every college needs landmarky nicknames to sound cool and be even more exclusionary though Will didn't know any of this yet. He just thought it was unusual to be walking around this big open square surrounded by big empty buildings all by himself.

Not even any of the other kids from Freshman Orientation were around, though technically, they should all have been heading in the same direction right about now, which didn't make Will feel any better about being On The Diag All By Himself. And so for the umpteenth time in as many seconds, he looked down at his campus map.

But, of course, the wily framers of the Freshman Orientation program knew they only had two days to strip all incomers of any semblance of self-confidence, and one of the very best ways to do this was to design a campus map that would have made Lewis and Clark late for Freshman Chem. So Will, who had never been great with directions to begin with, gave his own map a quarter turn. And then another. And then returned it to its easily accessible hiding place (so nothing could tag him as a foreigner) and stepped off toward one of the big empty buildings, still guessing but at least striding with confidence, just in case anyone might be watching. But the only ones really watching were the campus squirrels, who were alarmed less by a lack of navigational savvy than a lack of proffered peanuts.

Though even they could spot a Frosh.

For Will had recently made the biggest mistake of his young life. He had graduated from high school. He had then compounded his error by enrolling in the college of his choice, reverting to that state he had spent four long years evolving beyond, downgrading his classmen prefix from upper to lower and totem position from top-most to get-off-me-I-can't-breathe in the hope of securing some undefined and unguaranteed Better Good and now found himself paying for this hubris (more on this later) by wandering all by himself in a vastly unfamiliar space armed only with a map whose function, if you could figure it out, was to lead you *away* from its central "X".

And it was hot out, too.

Sweaty hot. Though the heat alone couldn't account for all the beads now forming rank on Will's brow. At least it looked cooler inside this building. From where Will was standing. Which was outside. Inside *anywhere* looked better as far as Will was concerned. So he quickly shored up his irresolution with another glance at his already thoroughly glanced-at map and then tucked it away again to put his hand on the handle of the glass door and pull sharply and...

Now even the squirrels gave up on him – or maybe it was just the sudden CLUNK! of the door refusing to open which caused them to flee, followed by the rat-a-tat rattle of the lock. And the next door was no better. Yielding the same result. That being that it wouldn't open.

Yes, it seemed that things involving *locks* were going to be a big problem for Will.

Since no one else was around, it was left to the symbolically-verdant (meaning "green") trees to witness Will's reluctant retrieval of his near-useless map, his journey to yet another glass door, and his sudden surprise (not to mention sheepish surveillance for campus security) when it opened.

The saplings must have thought it odd, if they could think, that someone would be trying so hard to break into the Natural History building.

There, almost, not quite, just down the hall a little actually, Will quickly found the room he had been looking for.

Double-checking its number against a slip of paper and finding the door handle mercifully rotatable, that is to say, not inhibited by a "lock", he settled himself with a deep breath, getting as full of it as he could, certain in the knowledge that he was not about to swing open a mere door but sort of like be turning a page if pages opened this way onto a new chapter of his *life*; that he was about to metamorph (which is a lot like "metaphor" rearranged with an extra "m" or "M" thrown in which doesn't mean much right now but will later) yes, metamorph from the warm but waning assurance of childhood's cocoon to the gossamer ascendance of young adulthood – with its promise of *caveat faux zeitgeist* and elegiac Ur-horizons and other things literary – that he was indeed about to enter...

Scene 2: Registration

Nope.

I'm going back to First Person.

For good.

For one thing, that Third Person stuff requires a certain facility and even familiarity with technique in order to achieve some semblance of flow, which is often called "prose".

Put another way, Third Person takes writing talent.

So for another thing, it's way hard to fake. You tend to want to get a little showy as you go on and end up pretentious and irritating, which is about as good a definition of "omnipotent" as any, I guess.

And finally, and this is probably the most important thing, at the end there, when Will was opening the door, remember?, I was going to have him discover that he had spent all that time and effort tracking down – are you ready...?

A janitorial closet. Sort of a comedic reversal sort of thing. But besides being weak, there's an even bigger problem with that. Namely:

It never happened.

I was just going to throw that in as a joke, something to counteract the effect of words like "Ur", which I don't even know what it means but I've seen before in books written in the Third Person because nobody would ever use a word like that in a real conversation and I sure as heck have never heard it spoken out loud and if I did I'd assume it was a stammer.

In other words, there was no Truth to it.

Now like I said before, I'll let you know when that happens, when something veers away from The Truth, but I'm also going to try and keep that kind of stuff to a minimum. And who knows? By the time we get to the end of the story...?

The Truth may even be enough.

The bottom line is, Third Person was leading us astray.

So I want to go back to "I".

But which "I"?

The "Me" I, or the "Will" I?

The "Me" I would be like the "I" in the Prologue, or now even, except that I'd have to try and make it a lot less annoying. Believe me, I know all this analysis is getting (if it hasn't already gotten) (maybe a long time ago) annoying. Because let's face it, too much introspection isn't any good (though personally, I don't mind). It's just that it's time to get to the dang story already.

That's why I'm leaning toward the "Will" I. That's the kid we left wandering around campus, lost, in the last chapter. Might as well give him a try. Besides, the "Me" I and "Will" I turn out to be almost exactly the same. And where they aren't...

I'll let you know.

So.

From now on, "I" will be Will talking, not Me.

And you might want to pay attention to this (last!) First Sentence, it's pretty character-revealing:

As usual, I didn't take the best way to get to where I wanted.

That's how I ended up the last freshman in line at C.R.I.S.P., which stands for Computer Registration Involving Student Participation, though a better idea of what it was really like would be if you crossed out the "Registration" and "Participation" and replaced it with "Reaming" and "Posterior".

But first frustrations first.

The place was crowded. The line wound up this big, wide staircase into Escher Infinity. And the building itself wasn't much to inspire confidence, either, seeming less founded on fine tradition than faded to institutionalism, an impression not helped by the UHF anxiety bouncing around off its cinder block walls, an echo of disoriented orienting freshpersons each chest-clutching two feeble shields of paper; an overworked worksheet and the almost talmudically thick "Schedule of Classes".

[Registration via paper products? What, is this a historical novel? You'll learn the Ugly Truth in Act 2, Scene 3: Fire Up It's Wednesday!]

It was kind of like standing in line for the big roller coaster at an amusement park you've never been to before; you were there voluntarily, it was something you had to do, maybe even wanted to do, but you couldn't help feeling like you'd rather be somewhere else right about now.

And the line just creeped. By the time I got to the top of the stairs and could see the actual C.R.I.S.P. room, all cracked and crumbling dark red brick and windows whose frames had been painted about a thousand times but never once stripped so that the paint grew thicker and thicker on the individual panes like hands slowly choking off all outside light, well, it felt less like I was about to enroll than be deloused.

There were a bunch of tables lined up along the outer perimeter of the chamber, circled like wagons, only with computers on top, with a bunch of people behind them whose function seemed to be to take handwritten worksheets from recent high school graduates, peck at keyboards, pause, then utter a few words that somehow doubled gravity in the vicinity of the hopeful's shoulders, eventually presenting this newly minted freshperson a quickly printed schedule and a credit or two less innocence with the hearty welcoming cry of "Next!".

Basically, this was the place you came to have underpaid-overworked counselors wielding computers like nightsticks tell you that every class you wanted to take in college wasn't available to you.

"You taking Band?"

It was the kid in line behind me. He was looking at my worksheet.

"Well, I..."

I wanted to say, no, not really, I had just scribbled "Band" down as a possibility, a wish really, and that I didn't really intend on signing up for it. Instead I said:

"Uhhh..."

Yeah, I really talk like that. Which is to say, never like I really intend to. Which is why I'm trying to write all this stuff down instead.

“You know, if you want to, you can sign up now and just drop it if you don’t make the audition. That’s what I’m gonna do.”

“Oh. Well. Hm...”

Fortunately, I was spared having to come up with any more noncommittal filler by an unexpected cry of “Next!” beckoning me to the next available--

No, actually, the conversation just ended with my “Hm...” and me turning back to face the front of the line and wait. That’s more The Truth, which is almost always less dramatically perfect than you want it to be, but...

Anyways, I waited a while until I really was “Next!”, and then headed for the chair just vacated by a paler, but CRISPer freshperson, putting my hopes in the hands of a professional hope crusher. It would be best, I suppose, if I could describe the counselor now keyboarding my worksheet of dreams into the school’s computer banks, but The Truth is I don’t even remember if it was a guy or a girl, let alone what he or she looked like. Let’s just use “she” for convenience (and because there’s probably going to be a lack of this particular pronoun in most of what follows).

So, “she” typed and I sweated.

And by the time I heard a dog-pitched

BEEP!

yelp out of her computer, it straightened me up in my seat like the rifle shot that killed Bambi’s mom.

But something was wrong. The counselor was frowning, then leaning in closer to her screen. Squinting. No, peering. Peeeeeeering.

Then more keystrokes. And more beeps. Until finally, she accepted defeat and settled back in her chair to deliver the head-shaking news:

"You got all your classes."

"I did?"

Her apologetic shrug clearly said, "Hey, it happens."

I wasn't going to argue. You learn not to ask too many questions when things are going your way. So I reached out to gather my worksheet but--

"Wait a minute..."

--she beat me to it. Something had caught her eye.

"...what's this?"

What? What's what?

"'Ensemble 101'. Did you want to try to add this?"

Whoa. Good question.

And for the first time, I myself had to settle back.

In doing so, my eyes finally drifted from the vent holes in the back of her computer to find, on the wall at the extreme of my periphery, a shoe. Not a real shoe, of course, but a picture of a shoe. A highly polished, dress black shoe with a flap of white leather snap-buttoned around it, covering the laces. This shoe was connected to a leg enrobed in stiff canvas with shiny outside pant seam, all bent at a protractor-perfect right angle at the knee, the toe pointed plumb-perfect to earth. The other leg stood strong and straight at attention, while the head of this impossibly-perfect poser was sliced into anonymity beyond the peak of a glossy poster – labeled with but a single word in large block:

"B A N D".

Also known as Ensemble 101.

"Did you want to try to add this?"

I looked at the poster. It was a sign. I mean, not just a sign-sign, but--

"Did you – want – to try – to add this?"

Like a (mildly irritated) call to destiny.

And so finally – hearing, seeing, *feeling* the call – I rose up and did what I've always done when confronted with Stark Opportunity.

"No."

Scene 3: Audition

So what was I doing here?

Standing on the steps of a place called "Reveille Hall", instrument case in hand?

Sweating again, that's what.

A few weeks had gone by since Freshman Orientation, but summer was saving its best for last. It wasn't the heat, though, that kept me from ascending to the doors at the top of the steps, it was the sight of all these other... well, not kids, really, students maybe, though some looked like they should already be running companies or something. They were everywhere, and for the first time it really pit-gutted me that I was a Freshman all over again.

I watched them streaming by me like flood water around some stump about to slip beneath the surface. Just standing there, clinging to shallow roots. Looking up at the big doors that led inside this "Reveille Hall" place, which was sort of like a miniature version of the Supreme Court, only without the tons of marble and lawyers.

But there would be judges.

Oh, there would be plenty of judges.

So what was I doing here?

Well, it's not that I actually changed my mind and registered for Band or anything, it's just that in the long, slooow summer weeks that followed Freshman Orientation, I kept wondering, and wondering, and what the heck? You didn't have to actually sign up for Band to audition; you could do that later.

If you made it.

So far, I had made it to the top of the stairs. And as I forced myself to take that last step, the first step inside, and suddenly confronted the reality of an entire rehearsal hall built entirely for an ensemble that used it only four months out of the year, I had to acknowledge there was another, more concrete, reason for being here.

Fear.

For this acousti-tiled temple had been erected solely for the glorification of "Band" – and here "Band" was synonymous with "Marching Band" and if you could make it here you could--

"Oof!"

I ran into a wall.

Or, I thought it was a wall – it was big and hard and unmoving – until I looked up and it glared down with an expression that only evolved species (read: "upper classmen") can give to lower while deciding whether it's worth the effort to swat.

"Sorry..."

That was me, obviously, not him. True, he had a mouth, but if he opened it I was pretty sure it wouldn't be to talk. Luckily, he decided to conserve his energy, sliding by me with the grace of a tectonic plate, then joined a herd of his fellows who greeted him like the long-awaited return of a bull market. I made it a point to stay well outside the perimeter of their eyes.

Not that they were really looking, though. Or anyone else, for that matter. It was sort of like being the new grunt in 'Nam. Nobody wanted to get too close, too soon, just in case you didn't make it.

Looking on the bright side, it was nice to see all my fears had been well-founded.

TWEET!

"All right, listen up!"

It wasn't the whistle itself that frightened me, you get those in marching band, it was the way the conversational buzz died before the tweeting had even finished, like someone had thrown a switch.

A very well-trained switch.

The tweeter was a guy named Dom, last year's Drum Major, clearly destined to own-not-lease a corporate jet someday, and though we were only separated by a few class levels, it was now apparent to me that there were such things in the Einsteinian universe as teenage light-years.

Dom quickly assigned us to different audition areas by instrument, in and out of Reveille Hall.

I ended up in the central rehearsal area with the largest group, all of us preparing for the inevitable. This was accomplished mainly by shuffling our feet and avoiding the chairs in the center of the room. Even so, the veterans were easy to spot, congregated as they were in uneasy pockets of bravado, while everyone else pretty much suffered alone.

Dom eventually instructed the veterans to move the chairs into a peculiar pattern, and there followed a brief flurry of dragging and scrapping until a giant circle had been formed with but a single chair-width gap – a wood and metal Stonehenge constructed by grim band druids with one particularly mysterious feature:

All the seats faced *outward.*

At first, I couldn't figure it out. But by the time Dom labeled the chairs on either side of the gap "first" and "last", then instructed us to take a seat along the circle in the approximate position we thought we warranted – and the rush for instrumental real estate began, I understood what was about to happen:

I was about to participate in the largest game of musical chairs ever played.

Picking where to sit wasn't really a hard decision. I just headed to the tail end of the circle with most of the rest of the newcomers. Everybody settled in pretty quickly, and the next thing I knew instrument case latches were going off like a barrage of gunfire.

My own case had only one latch that still popped crisply, the other having succumbed to mechanical fatigue long ago and now had to be coaxed open with a certain subtle wiggle that was more effective to unauthorized entry than its lock. Which didn't work anyway.

Resting the case on my lap as I had a thousand times before (more probably) I noted its rounded edges as I had a thousand times before (maybe a little less). Most other cases had square corners, sharp and defined. Mine were sloped and meandering, and like the case lid itself, nicked and scuffed and covered with the remnants of stickers I had put there as a kid over a decade ago, beat-up psychedelic flowers and slogans of "Love" and "Peace" or "...ove" and "Pea..." that really didn't belong anymore but I didn't have the heart to peal off.

Inside, it wasn't much better.

Bright red velvet was worn and crushed from wear and pressure, and the once cushy inside cover now formed a permanent negative impression of the top of the instrument, like the mold of a deathmask. And the instrument...

Ah, the instrument.

Legacy purchased at the expense of its luster.

But it hadn't always been that way...

Elementary School.

Like most kids, I started playing an instrument in about the 4th grade. This meant applying the full force of 9-year-old logic to the optimal choice of what to play. To me it was obvious.

In your typical elementary school band, you had your percussion section, which meant basically snare drum and bass which were inevitably less played than assaulted which I thought was dumb.

Then there was the woodwind section, primarily flutes – no way – and reeded instruments like sax and clarinet whose distinction didn't really matter because they both ended up playing the exact same note which was SQUEAK! and which I thought was stupid.

Then there was the brass section. Bright. Shiny.

Loud.

Which I thought was Cool.

But this still left some choices. The tuba wasn't even really a candidate, for one thing because I wasn't fat, which seemed to be an unspoken prerequisite, and because it seemed to have about a two-note range – low and lower – and because I could never disassociate it with words like "tragic" and "accident".

Trombone was a little different. Now, these guys *thought* they were Cool, and could at least fake it, but how cool could you really be with an overgrown version of the whistle you used to get in Cracker Jacks?

No, there was only one Truly Cool instrument in band. The only instrument I ever really wanted to play.

Trumpet.

Why would anyone pick anything else? All the notes in the world you could want right at your fingertips in just three little valves.

Of course, there was one catch.

Bl-a-a-a-a-a-t!

See, in any real trumpet, not just a toy one but a real one, to produce any kind of sound, you can't just blow.

Pw-a-a-a-fch!

You have to buzz.

Cr-aaaaaaaa-schlk!

It's hard to spell the – to be generous – "sounds" that come out of a trumpet the first time you pick one up and screw in the mouthpiece and press your lips to the cold metal ring and buzz. It's kind of like a rusty turboprop struggling to life on bad gas.

Except it takes years to gain any altitude.

Now, there's a reason for this. The French call it "embouchure", meaning "the position and use of the lips to produce a musical tone" – and besides being another reason to hate the French, "embouchure" was to become my personal demon in the trumpet years ahead.

But in the beginning, it was enough just to stumble onto a note. Which eventually did start to happen with some regularity. Two-note compositions from "Easy Steps To The Band" soon followed with gentle titles like "The Rocking Chair", and culminated in the four-note flurry of "Mary Had A Little Lamb" – an actual song!

I remember I used to just stare at my bright new shiny horn occasionally, thinking of the songs to come. The promise, the potential.

Back then, I could still see myself clearly reflected in its bell.

Music was all wide staffs and big round fluffy white notes.

Trumpet was simple.

But, of course, that couldn't last.

"Study the notes!"

Dom the Drum Major had made it to the end of the circle of chairs, slapping a small sheet of paper onto the stands in front of us. A sheet of paper with tiny narrow staffs nearly choked black with jagged-edged notes.

"Again, you'll play Intro to Letter B..."

I figured there must be at least 80 trumpets sitting around me here, and even if each one only took a couple minutes to audition--

"...then everyone will raise their hand to vote to see whether you move up or stay the same. Okay, here we go."

--I was in for a very long test.

"This is Chair #1."

Though the outward facing circle was designed to promote anonymity, I was sitting near the bottom and the best players were sitting near the top and the two ends circled around to almost meet at the gap, so I could easily glance over and see who "Chair #1" was.

I did so only once.

It was the Wall of Upperclassman I had bumped into earlier.

The next thing I knew, the Tornado Warning Siren went off – or that's what my eardrums told me until my brain was forced to override the sensation and concede that a wall of flesh and frown known only as "Chair #1" could somehow blow with such volume. And speed.

And hit *every* note.

God, what was I doing here?

I hated auditions. *Always* had.

Always...

Junior High.

After about five years of playing the trumpet, I had acquired a certain level of – okay, certain junior high level of – proficiency. This despite having also acquired more "bands" than a normal musician could handle, meaning, the kind that went around the teeth in what was then euphemistically labeled "Orthodontics" but was in actuality "Licensed Torture".

Ironically, the guy in the spotless white lab coat who used to stick pliers in my mouth every couple weeks wanted me to quit playing the trumpet, or take up a different instrument. Probably because he didn't like missing out on anything that fell under the category of "oral pain".

But I had made 2nd chair trumpet in 9th grade band, and while the inside of my lip often verged on ground chuck, I was content.

Of course, that couldn't last.

Why? Once again, the shadowy specter of graduation.

The *high* school band director swooped right into our junior high band class to audition prospects, in a little practice stall in the back. One by one they entered and one by one they emerged, always relieved, it seemed to me, to return to the chairs they had reluctantly abandoned, like chicks returning to the nest after a nudged first flight. They did all make it back, but in varied states of ruffled plumage. For as everyone knew, even Nature doesn't guarantee a 100% return.

This gave me plenty of opportunity to experiment with just the right chemical mix of fear and dread as I vicariously rehearsed for my own solo flight.

"Will Todd?"

Will I indeed.

I couldn't really ignore the guy, there were too many other kids – especially those who had already gone – who would finger me. So I left my 2nd chair trumpet in 9th grade band position and walked around to the back. Boy, these practice stalls were tiny, I had never really been in one before, and just looking inside I could tell my plan of playing so soft that maybe he couldn't hear me and would just assume I was doing it right wasn't going to fly.

"Hi, Will. I'm Mr. Douglass. Come on in and have a seat."

He seemed nice enough. Bald guy in probably his 40's (it's hard to tell in junior high when you really haven't noticed all that many people in their 40's) with way out of style black-rimmed glasses (the kind I wore) and a body like that cartoon guy who used to hang around with Popeye and would do anything for a hamburger. I definitely would have ran out to get him one to call this whole thing off. He seemed nice enough. Dark slacks, white short-sleeved dress shirt, no threatening buckles or insignia.

"Don't worry, I'll try to make this as painless as possible. Why don't we start with a warm-up...?"

He seemed nice enough.

"C scale – two octaves."

Straight for the jugular.

What you have to understand is, high "C" is the theoretical limit on a standard B-flat trumpet – made even more theoretical by the fact that I had never hit one before.

Never.

Not in going-on six years of playing the trumpet.

I started with the lower scale. No problem. I excelled at the lower notes. Even moving through middle "C", tuning note, I was fine, and celebrated by taking a breath. It was about at "F" that things typically started getting dicey for me. Not that I couldn't hit it, of course, I could, just not *consistently*. Ditto the "G", or "high G" (since it was above the staff), an "open" note, meaning no valves were depressed, and since there were more notes on the trumpet that could be hit with open valves than any other fingering, there were more chances to "slide off" to a lesser note. Fortunately, that didn't happen. Even though the "G" in question sat right on top of the staff, making it often tantalizingly just beyond my reach, I managed to squeeze one out on my way into uncharted territory. The next note, high "A", was a note I had never hit anywhere but by myself and unpreceded by any other notes and under just the right atmospheric conditions. I knew if I was to have any chance at it at all, I would have to apply some serious pressure. Now, I'm not talking about mental pressure here (there was no need to apply any more of that), but physical pressure, using both arms to pull the horn against my mouth with sufficient force to allow tiny fatiguing lip muscles to vibrate at 440,000 cycles per second. The frequency of high "A". (I looked that one up.) This was not unusual, by the way. Most junior high level trumpet players use a lot of arm pressure to reach the high notes. I'd seen guys peel off mouthpieces and leave rings so dark and deep you could hang a wreath from their lip. And high "A" was typically the note where you needed to start this brute force approach. Unfortunately, I had started back on "F". By the time I got to "A" I was already hurting. I used to wear wax on my braces to protect my inner lip as much as possible from the inexplicably razor-sharp steel corners of the hardware on my two front teeth, but past a certain point of pressure, the metal pushed right through. Like a knife through a candle. I was at that point. And hadn't even gotten to high "B" yet, a note I may have hit once by accident while noodling around but was too stunned to be sure and certainly couldn't repeat. Well, this time there was no doubt. I nailed it. And I had a witness, too. A witness credentialed by the School Board. I'm not sure what was going on. I remember holding onto my trumpet for dear life, like I was hanging from a cliff: High "A" was fingered with first (index) and second (middle) fingers, high "B" with just second finger, and high "C" – if I got there, to the summit – would be another open note, no fingers at all. It was like slowly letting go of a death grip – letting free – to reach up as an act of faith to the highest point I had ever dared for in my life. And no amount of adrenaline, no amount of arm pressure, no amount of nerve damage to my upper lip--

"CCCCCCCCCC!"

--could explain the Miracle of that moment.

"Okay, let's hear some of your prepared piece."

Obviously, the high school band director had heard high "C" before.

But I hadn't.

Not from *my* trumpet.

Still light-headed, I dabbed at my upper lip with the cuff of my shirt, then spread sheet music onto the stand in front of me – and in doing so, noticed the little red spots now on my sleeve.

It was the only high "C" I ever hit.

Ever.

And that's The Truth. It set me up in the top band in high school. It was not only the highest note I ever played, but the highest point of my entire trumpet career.

And all it had cost was a little blood...

"Show of hands?"

For about the 40th time back in Reveille Hall, some of us raised our hands and some of us didn't, and some trumpet found out how high he was going to go in Band.

"Next."

Even though the braces were long gone, I still had the habit of dabbing at my lip when I was nervous and carrying my horn. And we were only a little more than halfway through the circle of auditions. The same piece, over and over and over again. It was like listening to a train approach. In G major.

And being tied to the tracks.

Now maybe you're wondering how it could be so bad. After all, by this time, didn't I have *years* of experience? Yes, I did. Nine, to be exact. Almost a decade of playing the trumpet. With a fair number of auditions along the way.

So why the agony?

Well, I guess there's one thing I haven't told you yet.

Look at the guy's trumpet case next to me. On the floor. Sitting open. See those medals pinned inside? With the ribbons?

Blue and red...

High School.

After nine full years of playing in public school it had come down to this:

2nd chair, 1st trumpet, symphony band.

And I deserved it. I had good tone, strong technique, and a real ear for music. It was the best I could have possibly done.

Given my shortcomings.

A perfect way to illustrate would be that staple of high school band repertoire, "2nd Suite in Military F" by Gustav Holst. If you ever played in a high school ensemble, you know this song. It starts out with low (read: "inferior") brass doing a quick 5-note ascending run, echoed at least an octave up by high (read: "inconsequential") woodwinds. It only takes a few seconds, four taps of the foot, and then the real brass (read: "trumpets") take over, beginning with the same 5-note run but continuing up along the scale (a "G" scale because there's an F-sharp in there – a *high* F-sharp) and culminating in high "A", the exclamation point and pinnacle of the phrase.

Which I never hit.

Ever.

Instead, I would play the run leading up to the high "A" and rest, or lay off when the time came, allowing the 1st chair trumpet to nail the big boy. Which was why he was 1st chair trumpet and I never would be. See, there were two main areas that I had trouble as a trumpet player:

Endurance and Range.

Compare these to the two main attributes most prized by trumpet players:

Range and Endurance.

And I can tell you exactly why I didn't have them. Physically, at least. Cosmically, the question has never really been answered to my satisfaction. In any case, it's the one thing I haven't told you yet. Prepare yourself. Here it comes.

I have no upper lip.

Trumpetically speaking, that is. The most vital part of a trumpet player's anatomy, and I had little more than an *allegation* of an upper lip. It's as if you went straight down from my nose across the still barren mustache plateau and – BOOM – right to the bottom lip. But it's the *upper* lip that does the important buzz work in a mouthpiece. No upper lip?

No range.

No endurance.

There were in fact many implications to this freakish lack of anatomy, several of which concerned the specter of kissing, but as far as the trumpet was concerned, the most important implication was this:

I couldn't hit – every – note.

Now, that's not so bad when you're playing in a group. You're covered. Like the high "A" in "Second Suite in Military F".

But there's one place it doesn't work.

"You ready for Solo?"

1st chair trumpet. Just making conversation. A nice guy, really, a little full of himself, but why shouldn't he be after somehow being born with a double portion of upper lip, at least one of which might have been mine (an observation that fueled elaborate mind-movies in which I often indulged full teen martyrdom).

He was referring to the statewide "Solo and Ensemble Festival".

Something I had silently but proudly managed to avoid for nine years.

It was an annual chance to pay a fee to have people you've never met before and would never meet again sit and tell you how bad you played.

If, however, your performance was somehow judged "excellent", you were awarded a medal. A medal with a blue ribbon. A red ribbon was for "good".

1st chair trumpet had plenty of ribbons pinned inside his case.

A few red, mostly blue.

Red and blue...

It's hard to oil your valves when your hand is shaking.

I had now heard the same piece played literally 70 times in Reveille Hall, the degree of mangalation (which ought to be a musical term) increasing as the audition fuse burned down to the bottom of the circle and my own turn drew nearer. I had followed along and fingered the notes so often that not only could I have played them by heart (a skill of no value here), but my valves were starting to stick.

Valve oil comes in a variety of brands and containers, the majority a greasy yellow liquid in a small plastic bottle that most guys just stick nozzle first into the little hole at the bottom of each valve and squeeze with all their might. I preferred "Fast Al Cass" valve oil because it was clear and "Odorless!" and came in a little glass bottle with its own eye dropper that required some finesse and because it was more expensive so it was at least perceived as a premium thing.

And because I needed every advantage I could get.

Usually, I would unscrew my trumpet's valves individually at the top, letting the oil drip down around each unblemished silver cylinder. These were machined marvels, drilled through with mysteriously canted tunnels for rechanneling the flow of air, precisely and consistently, whenever pressed.

How I envied them.

But there was no longer any time for careful lubrication. The guy just two chairs up from me was auditioning. I turned my horn over, targeting the small holes in the bottom valve caps. But now even Fast Al Cass, whom I had known for almost half my life, betrayed me, the eye dropper proving too unstable to manage in a hand shaking at nearly the frequency of high "A".

It was horrible, really. Because the thing was, I had been at this extreme once before; felt like this in one other place.

And I knew how it was going to turn out...

Solo and Ensemble Festival.

A year earlier. My luck had finally run out. One year shy of never having to face the threat of the Festival again, a well-respected and unwanted private instructor who played 1st trumpet in a professional orchestra (now defunct) and had the kind of upper lip that Ringling Brothers scouts for and taught most of the trumpet players I knew in school for six bucks a half hour, had insisted I prepare a piece like all his other students did for the Solo and Ensemble Festival.

So I did.

Because I was still a kid and you did what you were told. Because it was easier than fighting.

Because I was stupid.

It was a classic solo trumpet piece I can't remember the name of, maybe because I blocked it, lots of movement and double-tonguing, which I was actually pretty good at. In fact, I could play just about everything in the piece.

In pieces.

Meaning I could handle sections as long as I could take rests in between and not have to confront my twin demons of Range and Endurance.

Unfortunately, you can't actually signal "time out" during a solo.

So I knew what was coming.

The Festival was held at some high school upstate. The room was cramped and covered floor to ceiling in dingy white sound-absorbing tile with disquieting smudges, kind of like solitary confinement at an insane asylum. Only with a piano.

Fact: There's no way to produce an audible tone when the relative humidity of the inside of your mouth is at 0%.

There were chairs facing the piano. And me. A row of half a dozen seats, six shy of a jury box. Three held judges, whom I could no more look in the eye and describe now than I could then. The others were for spectators. Some girl was there. The 1st chair trumpet from my high school band was there.

My dad was there...

I can't. Forget it. I didn't get a blue ribbon or even a red. They didn't have a color for the level I performed at. Just forget it. It was too painful. One of the worst experiences of my life.

And I was about to repeat that experience right now.

The trumpet just before me was playing the audition piece. With extreme mangalation. Now, okay, it maybe wasn't really like being a grunt in 'Nam and watching the guy next to you get riddled with bullets while you're waiting to be next or anything but I swear I have at least an *idea* of what it must feel like to thousand-yard stare into the great gaping maw of Naked Terror.

In other words, I was a nervous wreck.

Worse, I was a nervous wreck with no upper lip.

Which brings us back to the question originally posed.

"Should he move up?"

The same question Drum Major Dom had been posing for 2½ hours now. Most often followed by:

"Next?"

Or, to put it in my own words, the words that were now screaming through my skull and cleaving deep into my brain folds:

What was I doing here!? Why? WHY was I doing this...?

And I think I have an honest answer.

I don't know.

My horn had never felt this heavy before. It was like some spatial anomaly with alien gravity was opening up around it, starting at the bell and ending at my chest. I tried to coax a little saliva into my mouth – no joy – and placed the mouthpiece against my lips (or "lip") anyway. Deep breath, or as deep as I could get with the alien gravity bearing down on my shoulders. There was no turning back now. The moment had come.

What was I doing here?

I stumbled into the Intro sounding pinched, rushed, and erratic. The word I would use is:

Uncertain.

But sometimes The Truth is simply that: You just don't know. I certainly couldn't have given you one good reason at the time what I was doing here. But even with the advantage of perspective, I'm still not sure. All I can do is offer several possibilities.

The 1st phrase consisted of two 16th-note runs that I should have been able to handle, but turned out to be:

Harder than I thought.

I mean, maybe I wasn't fully aware of what I was getting into. Maybe I kept a realistic consideration of it all walled off in the back of my mind, because I knew if I thought about it too much, I might not go through with it.

The 2nd phrase continued with more runs, more problems, or:

More of the same.

Meaning, maybe it simply had to do with the fact that I was uprooting my life to start college anyways, and what was one more gut-wrenching, psyche-threatening trauma to add to the list?

The next phrase was more or less a repeat of the first, which made things a little:

Easier.

In other words, maybe it was just the lesser of two evils. Maybe I would've always wondered if I could've made it, and somehow I knew that would be worse than actually finding out.

The 4th and final phrase was a long and ascending run ending in high "G". Or was supposed to end in high "G". I tried – repeatedly – to get there, but couldn't hold on, sliding off and sliding off like the desperate braying of a brass donkey.

Falling short, falling short...

What was I doing here?

Pick your phrase. Take your choice.

Me, I just slowly lowered my trumpet to half mast.

"Should he move up?"

Even I didn't vote for me.

"Next."

It was over.

I wouldn't move up...

...but I wouldn't move down, either.

Apparently, there were others just as skilled as I in the art of self-mangalation. Or maybe they were just bad trumpet players. One thing's for sure, after three hours of auditions with the same 20 seconds of music (that's right, just 20 seconds – that aforementioned spatial anomaly apparently had some temporal effects as well) played over 80 times in a row, this group wouldn't have raised a hand to vote for the abolition of campus anti-orgy laws.

And so by sheer, tenacious apathy--

"That's it."

--I ended up in the same chair I had chosen at the beginning. There was a lesson in there somewhere, but I missed it because of the number 74.

"All right, listen up. One through 75..."

My Chair Number was 74.

"...congratulations and welcome to the Band!"

The circle of musical doom immediately dissolved in a concerto of chair scraping, back slapping, and high fiving. Pent-up smiles were finally paroled from their prisons.

Gravity returned to 1g.

Even I got to share in some of the sudden camaraderie.

This is The Truth. I had made the Band by one chair. The hard part was over.

Or so I thought.

Until I noticed the corner of the room where Drum Major Dom had gathered those players who didn't make the cut, several of whom were staring back at me.

Hard.

My marching band story was only beginning...

Act Two: Hell Week

Scene 1: Fire Up It's Monday!

It was the week before school started. Actually, I guess I shouldn't call it just "school" anymore, it was "college" and if you wanted to get really pretentious about it, "university". The "U", as it was known. Though, to tell The Truth, it was more often referred to as the U "of M", because it was the university of, uh, the uh, university of the, or, the "M", uh... Ah, heck.

I'm talking here about the University of Michigan.

I'm talking about the University of Michigan because that's where I went to college, but if you'd rather think of it as someplace else, go ahead. I've been trying to keep things as generic as possible up until now, so everybody could relate to everything however they wanted, but there's one place where I have to get specific or you might not understand. See, at the University of Michigan, band wasn't just "Band", it was "The University of Michigan Marching Band". We even had our own acronym, and it didn't even need the "U":

M.M.B.

Michigan Marching Band. I bring it up because unlike maybe a lot of other places you might know about, our marching band, *the* marching band – MMB – was actually a respected institution on campus.

I know this is hard to believe.

But witness Reveille Hall.

Here was this multi-million dollar facility built exclusively for the use of a *marching* band. *The* marching band. MMB. It was located on South Campus, the athletic campus, miles away and measures apart from the other music school facilities on North Campus. It had a lobby, locker hall, equipment room, offices, and its own music library. It was state-of-the-art, built on the epauletted shoulders of marching immortals.

And alumni funds.

One of these immortals (now dead) was the guy the hall was named after, Dr. William D. Rev-- well, actually, his last name wasn't "Reveille", but it was awfully close, and I'm changing all the names in this story because (even though this particular guy is dead), I hear you can get sued for calling people by their actual names and I definitely don't need any of that and besides, it's not really important to get my ultimate point across. And it's real close anyway, like I said, to the actual name of the guy (who can't sue me because he's dead but I guess his relatives could) who lent his name to the building and used to be a Director of Bands, including the Michigan Marching Band, back in its formative days. He was a strict disciplinarian, but I know there are still alumni out there who fondly recall the beatings of his baton. So "Reveille Hall". Which is spelled for some reason (the French again, I believe) in a way that makes it hard to know how the word is pronounced, which is "REH-vel-ee", which is kind of nice because it's a trumpet thing.

And a call to action.

The point is, there was a lot to live up to here.

These things were not left to chance. Reveille Hall was filled with signs and slogans, many of which were set down in hand-painted permanency and dutifully hung around the central rehearsal room, a bright white fluorescent space big enough to accommodate 300 musicians (I'm including percussionists here). The signs ranged from the topical to the philosophical. One prominent one said: "Perfection is made up of trifles. But perfection is no trifle." It took 15 years before I found out this was a quote from the Renaissance artist Michelangelo, and not our Drum Major, Dom.

There was also a big wooden board on the front wall with a pair of feet marching in flames and the words, "Fire Up: It's..." followed by a blank slot in which the names of the days of the week could be (and would be – the board was never wrong) inserted to let you know how close you were to that all-important day of the week, Saturday. Game Day. Which seemed inefficient to me, taking out and putting in little slats of brightly painted wood every morning, though I suppose it did give each day its own distinctive color. It was as if inside Reveille Hall we followed our own non-Gregorian calendar, the "Fire Up" calendar. Where every day of the week had its own exclamation point painted on for emphasis.

Today was "Monday!"

Our first rehearsal. My first rehearsal here ever. Yesterday, I had been just another kid trapped in the limbo between high school and college. Today, I was a member of one of the best (actually, I threw in that "one of" for modesty) marching bands in the country, and apparently a full member as well, seeing that we rookies weren't required to wear any special identification or anything.

MMB.

The Michigan Marching Band.

If it hadn't been for not having a clue as to what was going to happen next, I might have actually enjoyed the buzz.

Most of this was coming from the roughly 274 other people around me. It was the first time since auditions that everybody had been in the same room together, only now everybody had their own seat. Even me. Chair 74 out of 75 in the trumpet section, the largest (by far) of any section in the band. All the activity going on was a little overwhelming: Assistants handing out music, slapping sheets to stands; Section Leaders presiding over rows of instruments I had never seen before; Returnees trying to pretend all this was nothing special, but voices a little too loud; Newcomers afraid to speak at all, and not bothering to pretend; Proximity Players with foreign warm-up routines and all of it all around me buzzing and blowing and drumming and *thrumming* a dizzying crescendo of anticipation.

Our first piece thus seemed to me an undirected Symphony in Cacophony, a primal monaural stew that somehow had to develop lungs and legs and evolve into a precision musical marching entity.

In less than a week.

How could this possibly come to pass? It would take an act of god, a supreme being who wielded the supreme power to wring out of this supreme chaos, a Band. It would take--

"Everybody up!"

--George R. Cavendish.

The command came from Dom the Drum Major, and meant exactly what it said. No matter where you were, no matter what you were doing, you got to your feet.

Fast.

Actually, “rocket to attention” might be a better descriptor, as the eerily synchronous SCRAPE! of over 200 chairs blew a giant punctuation mark through the jet drone that had filled the room, snuffing it into absolute silence. And rigidity. Everybody statufied, ramrod straight, their instruments magnetized into uniform polarity, and I made sure I fumbled mine into an approximation. This was no time to stand out. Even Dom, waiting a discreet step back from the podium, looked a little nervous, unable to keep the furrow out of his brow as he glanced to the door. It was like catching your normally unflappable Master Sergeant stop dead in his tracks to scan the top of a hill, suddenly straining to hear. Only it stays quiet.

Too quiet.

Something was definitely headed our way. And whatever it was--

“Shh!”

(Someone had coughed.)

--it was about to make an Entrance.

And then it did.

Remember that first scene in “Patton”? Where George C. Scott climbs up in front of that giant American flag? And then word-strafes his own troops with a few unvarnished growls of introduction?

Well, remove Patton’s helmet and whiten and wizen the face a bit to more closely approximate Moses arriving with the stone-carved holy word of god almighty – only with his hair cropped short and the excess glued to his eyebrows – and you're about ready to receive from Mount Podium, as we did, the following benediction:

"Now... I want you to remember... that no one ever won a spot in this Band... by giving less than 150 percent. They won it... by letting the other poor dumb bastard give less than 150 percent."

George – R. – Cavendish.

Well, okay, maybe he didn't say "bastard", but you get the idea.

What he definitely *did* say, though, was "150 percent". It was the most important and oft-used slogan in all of MMB--

"Give 150 percent!"

--and while mathematically impossible nonetheless framed Cavendish every time he stepped up to the music, letters towering in unambiguous black-and-white on a foreboding placard behind him.

Historical Note:

Somewhere back in the mists of marching antiquity, Cavendish had been Reveille's hand-picked successor. They were, in fact, the only two directors who had conducted the Michigan Marching Band *for the last half century.* Thus, when Cavendish approached his six inch carpeted podium and slowly and deliberately raised his twelve inch ivory baton, both the long-acquainted and newly-converted amongst us expected miracles.

In short:

Cavendish was the Burning Bush of Marching Band.

When he spoke, you took off your shoes and listened:

"B-flat concert."

Which in the codified language of music orthodoxy meant "tuning note". It also meant that for the first time I was surrounded by the sound of 274 instruments playing in concert, embedding me in a mixed frequency force field strong enough to make the hairs on my arm stand up.

Actually, it was more like being inside an aural cotton ball, for even with its raw power, the sound less battered than swaddled. Like a sonic security blanket. But the tingle lasted only briefly. The baton that had given breath of life to our B-flat concert now took it away.

That was the power of Cavendish.

A flick of the wrist - a bolt of words:

"Trumpets! One at a time."

Of course, from a terror standpoint, this was only slightly better than waiting to perform an entire audition piece, but I got through it, managing even not to crumble to dust under the direct glare of Our Director, which must have lasted upwards of 5 seconds.

And despite the fact that I was pretty sure I had given less than 150%.

And so, as we proceeded through each section, instrument by instrument, one by one, tuning individually, we all simply accepted the fact from On High that we would spend our entire first rehearsal playing just one note apiece.

Cavendish'll become particularly important at the climax of the story. But like most vertically-integrated theocracies, you rarely have direct contact with the guy at the top. Instead, there are layers of mid-shepherdment, whose job it is to keep the lambs from getting lost...

Baaaaaa.

I am lost.

It's a few hours later and I'm out on "Elbert Field", named after the guy (dead) who wrote our fight song and which isn't a field at all but a parking lot next to a field with yard lines painted onto the asphalt instead of spaces and which is used for all marching rehearsals.

Right now I'm performing that universal prerequisite to marching, which is wandering, nose buried in a chart that shouldn't be this hard to figure out and copied onto legal-sized paper (the first time I've ever seen any) because the Michigan Marching Band is just too big to fit onto standard 8½ by 11.

At least I'm not the only one still looking for their spot.

Though more and more people are falling into line while I'm still on the outskirts searching for a place to stand.

Okay, don't panic, let's do this again. Here's "Todd, Will", Chair Number 74... (This is the only time, by the way, my name ever appears on a chart. From here on out, I'm just a dot with a number next to it.) Okay, so Chair Number 74 corresponds to this other number 82 which, see Chart "B", according to these dots should put me in about the middle of the most important formation in all of marching band...

The Block.

An impressive assemblage of human rows and columns, laid out by yardline.

This was where you drilled.

This was where you paraded.

This... was home.

And like all homes, the quality of life depended on the neighborhood. My new address was "Rank 8", which was eight rows

– or “ranks” – back from the front of The Block, easy enough, one, two, three, four, five, six, seven... Nope, wait a minute, this can’t be right. I recognize the guys in this row, all hanging out much too casually and everywhere but the yardline, charts rakishly tucked into their sweat socks. These were all *1st* trumpets. Upperclassmen. Seniors, for god’s sake. Obviously not right. I must’ve miscounted. One, two, three, four, five, six, seven... I can’t believe this. This is actually kind of disappointing. My first day, my first appearance on a chart in a major college marching band and *I'm a misprint*. Had to be. I’d better find somebody in charge, though I’ll have to put this delicately; now where’s...?

“Why aren’t you in your place?”

Ah, good, Dom the Drum Major, he found me instead. We’ll straighten this out.

“Uh, well...”

“What’s your Block Number?”

“Uh, well, according to <u>this</u>, um... 82, but...”

Dom took three quick steps into Rank 8.

“Right here.”

The way he pointed to that particular spot, like he knew every pebble in the asphalt even better than the back of his whistle, left no room for argument. I took up residence on my twelve inches of yardline, immediately coming under the scrutiny of those who could actually afford this neighborhood. I was a lone 3rd trumpet amongst a rank that was exclusively 1st, and from the extremes of my peripheral vision I could see them all calculating the sudden plunge in property values.

Now, some people I guess would've been thrilled to be accorded a place in the Band's premiere rank. But I was odd man out. Waaaaay out. If this was Trumpet Valhalla, I was Loki, God of the Lipless.

Jeez, where was Thor when you needed him?

"Hi. I'm Thor."

Tall. Long blond hair. No hammer, but generally god-like. Everything, in fact, I wasn't. And now smiling down at me beneficently:

"You 82?"

"Uh, well, according to this, um... yes, but..."

"I'm 81. Welcome to Rank 8."

Okay, The Truth: The guy's name wasn't really "Thor". It was George. And he didn't actually look the way I just described him, either. But we're going to leave him "Thor" because when he stretched out his hand to take mine, it was like being pulled from a vast sea storm of uncertainty by the thunder god himself and shown the first step on the rainbow bridge to Asgard. Which, truthfully again, is overstating it a little.

But only a little.

TWEET!

"Let's go – everybody find your rank! Move it, move it, *move* it...!"

Dom the Drum Major again. And though I, 82, had found my rank – at least, apparently – I still tensed just in case I had to "move it".

But Thor only grinned:

"Just hang loose. Things won't start getting ugly until the *second* whistle."

Thor, 81, helped me to see what did – and more importantly – what didn't have to be taken seriously. 83, on the other hand...

"Oh, so sorry, you must be of this height to ride this attraction."

Charlie Gupta. Who didn't take *anything* seriously.

Charlie was Hindu, with enough upper lip to play 1st trumpet *and* sport a mustache, and was currently chopping the air just above my head to be sure Thor and I were getting his joke. Thor allowed another grin:

"Chuckles, this is the young lad who'll be keeping us apart this year."

"Oh, no, Norse-god. For no Newbie - clearly no offense is intended – can or will interrupt our ultimate duet, no matter who has given him a Block Number that says so otherwise."

"*Cavendish* assigns all Block Numbers."

"Welcome to Rank 8."

Charlie helped keep alive the hope that in some future I could not yet fathom, big-time college marching band might actually be--

TWEEEEET!

--non-bladder-threatening.

The second whistle. Now even Charlie and Thor snapped to attention. I did the same, looking side-to-side like a toddler trying to imitate his older brothers. Better than older brothers, these were the #2 and #3 trumpets in band, literally, the second and third chairs of the entire trumpet section – flanking the 74th. With each of them carrying a gleaming silver horn to my weathered brass, it was kind of like being that layer of a newly struck coin the U.S. Mint doesn't like to talk about.

Which was fine with me.

Because it was also like being *inside* something. Covered. Protected. So when Dom the Drum Major loudly announced in that most weathered instrument of his own:

"Listen up! Anyone who has *not* found their rank – speak now!"

I almost grinned.

I had found my place in The Block.

All I had to do was follow my bookends to stay out of trouble. They had been doing this for three years apiece. They were the best that Band had to offer.

"Rank Leaders!"

But I was wrong.

"Inspection!"

As good as they were...

THUMP!

...there was someone better.

THUMP!

Remember that scene in "Jurassic Park" where the T-Rex is coming but before you see him you see this cup of water on a dashboard ripple with his approach?

THUMP!

Well, it was the reflection of my own face in the bell of my own horn that I now saw rippling....

THUMP!

...before the creature's feet appeared on the asphalt before my lowered eyes, feet that brought their own threat of extinction with a final dino-sized

THUMP-THUMP!

They waited, less than an inch away from my own suddenly lilliputian toes, leaving me no choice but to slowly raise my eyes past gargantuan if barely mammalian legs the size of torsos that looked like something the Japanese had designed, you know, one of those transformer bots with fuel tanks that morphed into thighs. They seemed to attach directly to a chest the size of the Hindenberg, with lungs that could blow more wind than Congress. But now inflated with something much more volatile and explosive, as evidenced by a face that was as square and blunt and glowering as the presidents who didn't make the cut on Rushmore.

He was a tireless marcher.

He was a powerful player.

And to top it all off:

He hated my living guts.

For this was not an unfamiliar face. It was, in fact, the same face with roughly the same scowl that I had bumped into accidentally before auditions. The Upperclassman. And 1st Chair Trumpet.

And Rank Leader of my new home in The Block.

He was, quite simply:

"Marko."

It was Thor speaking. But Marko kept his eyes buried into my flesh.

"What."

"You're supposed to inspect me first."

Marko turned, but only his eyes, and only a fraction.

"You're at attention, Thor."

And if ever there was any doubt where authority lay in Rank 8, it was shattered by the snap of Thor's return to attention.

Marko's eyes were all mine again.

Truthfully, I was never to know exactly *why* Marko hated my living guts. I think it was just one of those whims of nature you couldn't explain, like twisters and trailer parks. I ran down several lines of thought, though.

For one thing, I was a Freshman. Everybody else in Rank 8 was an Upperclassman. And therefore older than me. Taller, too. At attention, I made our row look like a comb with a single broken tooth.

For another thing, I was a 3rd trumpet. Everybody else in Rank 8 was a 1st. Which made about as much sense as the London Philharmonic hiring in one of those guys who blows on a jug.

And for a last thing, while everybody else in Rank 8 was keeping cool...

"We don't wear 'pants' in the Michigan Marching Band... '(t)odd'."

Reading my last name off his chart, Marko somehow managed to spit away the first consonant while emphasizing the "odd". He was right about one thing, though, everybody else in Rank 8, wait, no, now that he mentioned it, the *entire Band*, was wearing shorts.

Except me.

Marko returned his glare to my pants of shame:

"*Especially...*"

Go ahead, say it, say it – Polyester!

"...during Hell Week."

I hadn't seen a slo-mo smirk like the one that grew on Marko's face since the Grinch tried to 211 Christmas, but at least he decided not to take away my doo-dinglers just yet and moved on to the next inspectee.

Though the words "Hell Week" continued to ring in my ears.

It was the first time I'd heard the phrase. It wouldn't be the last. It's very mention could strike terror into Band member's hearts.

"Marko, Marko, how does your garden grow?"

"Shut up, Charlie."

"Okay."

Well, most Band members, anyway.

And with good reason.

"Hell Week" was the week before classes began, the unofficial last week of summer and official last week of freedom on the student calendar. But for the Michigan Marching Band, it was more than just a way to mark time. It was the ticking clock we were all marching against, the time allotted to transform a block of raw, summer-vacation-bloated recruits into a precision marching machine.

It was torturous.

It was ungodly hot.

It was about five working days long.

It *was* Hell Week.

And it all started with...

Scene 1a: The Lock

"Everybody up!"

"One!"

"Everybody down..."

Our first lesson in marching was learning how to stand still.

"Everybody up!"

"One!"

"Everybody down..."

In other words, "at Attention".

Get your protractor ready, here's a check list:

45 degrees: The feet. Heels together, toes apart. Arches on the yardline.

90 degrees: The right arm. Elbow perpendicular to forearm, forearm perpendicular to the planes perpendicular to the symmetric axis of the body.

180 degrees: Everything else. Legs straight, spine straight, eyes straight ahead. Left hand straight down along left outseam.

And right hand balancing all these various angles to achieve...

"Everybody up!"

"One!"

"Everybody down..."

...the all-important "horn carry": Fingers wrapped around valve casing, bell facing earthward, mouthpiece pointing to heaven. The trumpet as musical weapon ready to be snap-rotated into gridiron action.

"Everybody up!"

"One!"

"Everybody down..."

But, of course, before we could really learn how to stand at Attention, which is to say, stand still, we had to learn how to stand *up*.

Which meant starting in a full crouch on the yardline, then blasting up to chisel-perfect Attention at the command of the Drum Major.

"Everybody up!"

"One!"

"Everybody down..."

Over and over *and over* again.

Now, I had been in marching band in high school. It was kind of fun. It was definitely loose. It was--

"Everybody up!"

"One!"

--assumed you already knew how to stand up.

"Everybody down..."

But this was the Michigan Marching Band – MMB – where nothing was taken for granted except giving 150% effort and...

"Everybody up!"

"One!"

...no grading on a curve.

"You're late! You're *late*! Where's the effort? *Where's* the effort...?"

Dom was headed right for me, so I used up one of my last oh-please-god-no coupons and he stopped just two ranks ahead, outdoing the wilt power of the sun on some other fractionally late riser who had compounded his error by accompanying it with a less than impending-death scream of "One!"

Which was what you yelled to let the Drum Major know you were following commands. And since there was only one distinct step to standing up – namely, standing up – you only yelled one thing – namely, "One!" – though "Up!" might have made more sense, given that "One!" holds a promise of "Two!" and standing up never involved a "Two!" so it seemed you were always waiting for something that would never come.

Which, in general, is not a very good policy. In life, that is. In Band, nobody questioned it. In Band, you did what you were told to do.

You were told to do a lot of things in Band.

"Attention by the numbers! Readyyyyy... one!"

"One!"

This was a different "One!".

Standing up into Attention isn't the same as being *called* to Attention. A marching band is called to Attention when they're already standing up, usually as a way to quiet everybody down and settle them into a formation.

Of course, Attention means different things to different bands. When I was in high school, it meant you could continue screwing around, but just do it less obviously for that period of time determined by the authority and proximity of the person screaming "A-ten-HUT, A-ten-HUT!" – though usually no longer than a few seconds. We also had this cute little three-step way of executing the command where you raised and lowered your left foot, kicked out with your right at a 45 degree angle in front of your body, then returned the right heel next to the left – all while shouting "One-Kick-Down!". Lift and Kick. At least, that was the theory. In practice, so long as your feet sort of lost contact with the ground, you were okay. On hot days, we just bent our knees a little.

Those were the days.

"No! *No*! Down! DOWN! This is the *Michigan* Marching Band, the *Michigan* Marching Band! Attention by the numbers! Readyyyyy... one!"

"ONE!"

Attention "by the numbers" meant you were supposed to stop and hold each step in the process until the Drum Major told you to move on to the next step by shouting the next number. This was the preferred teaching method for commands, since it allowed each step to be isolated and perfected.

And, of course, because it was more painful.

"You're moving, you're *moving*! Who's *moving*...?"

I was moving. It was hard not to when your left leg was raised unnaturally high into the air, thigh parallel to the ground, calf perpendicular, toe pointed earthward; trying to establish a teetering balance on your stiffening right leg while maintaining a perfect unwavering horn carry even though your instrument is cantilevered away from your body for maximum potential instability. It was the signature position of the Michigan Marching Band. The one I had seen on that poster at Registration.

How many years ago was that...?

"Two!"

"TWO!"

"Two!" was a whole different ball game. Now the legs changed – "like pistons" – the left driving down to support the weight while the right snapped up into its namesake angle. And even the veterans, who hadn't contorted themselves into these positions since last season, were now playing musculoskeletal Twister with the non-negotiable force of gravity. Fortunately, there was one part of "Attention by the numbers!" at which I excelled.

"Three!"

"THREE!"

"Three!" was where you got to put everything back down. And just stand there at Attention again, both feet hugging terra firma, glad to be someplace familiar.

Of course, that couldn't last.

For drilling "Attention" for over two hours was cake compared to what came next.

For what came next was what set the Michigan Marching Band apart from all others.

And what came next was what would set me apart from the Michigan Marching Band.

Because what came next was, ironically, the key to *un*-locking the Michigan Marching Band...

It starts out innocently enough.

Four – TWEET! – very – TWEET! – slow – TWEET! – whistles – TWEET! – trigger an

"UP!"

of all instruments synch-snapping into play-ready position – though there will be no playing in this drill, whose arming sequence continues on a single snare drum that takes over the Drum Major's whistle tempo with

four – BANG! – more – BANG! – preparatory – BANG! – beats – BANG! – accompanied by

"Sweep, sweep, sweep, sweep..."

undulating in hushed chant throughout the Band like a prayer before dying and climaxing with a final blown-chord wail of

"LOCK!"

whereupon The Story actually begins.

The Lock.

Here it is.

Here we go:

The left leg explodes upward into the precise angular "One!" of Attention – thigh parallel to the ground, calf perpendicular, toe pointed earthward – but with no stationary "Two!" to follow as the entire 275-member human Block finally abandons the security of the yardline and makes its first lurching move forward into the great void between, each step a sudden 90 degree angle at the knee, locked and held as long as possible until the next

BANG!

of the snare.

Not unlike the galley scene from "Ben Hur".

This was known as "sweeping the field", or more simply "Sweeps".

Sweeps were a conditioning drill. They were meant to build up muscle and wind while tearing down mental barriers like the will to protest.

And the more the snare pushed the tempo – and the snare always pushed the tempo – the harder it got. Because each Lock had to be distinct:

"Lock! – Lock! – Lock! – Lock...!"

"Change like a piston!"

"No bicycling!"

I think ideally what was supposed to happen was that your body was supposed to create a quantum physical anomaly between each locked leg position, so that there would be no physically discernable movement in between. Unfortunately, my freshman body couldn't sign up for quantum physics until sophomore year, so mostly, it was just confused and in pain.

Which is about as good a description of "The Lock" as any.

I suggest you give it a try. Really. Right now. Stand up – you can take the book with you, pretend it's a horn (although a pretty light one) – lift your left leg – faster! – thigh parallel to the ground, calf perpendicular, toe pointed earthward – then switch as quickly as possible to your right leg.

No bicycling!

No hopping!

Hey, YOU, change like a piston!

Repeat about a thousand times.

It's the only way I can think of to make you truly understand how the "Lock – Lock – LOCK...!", or as I used to put it the--

"Lock – (Pant) – Lahck – (Pant!) – Laghhh – (PANT...!)"

--put the "Hell" in "Hell Week".

Although for this particular week, there was another good reason.

This particular year, the week before classes started broke all records for heat. It got to the point that if it had dropped below 100 degrees, the Band would've huddled for warmth. We needn't have worried, though. For some thoughtful University committee had provided us a practice field with the most anti-reflective, sun-sucking surface known to man.

Tar.

I'm not kidding.

I can remember during one "break", down on one knee, my head resting on my mouthpiece, staring at a frighteningly flushed face in the bell of my trumpet while an arc weld Lawrence-of-Arabia sunspot vaporized any drops of sweat as soon as they hit the brass – and my whole reflection slowly sinking into the black ooze of "Elbert Field".

It was hot.

In fact, resting too long put the whole Band in danger of becoming the world's biggest Roach Motel: They march in, but they don't march out.

"Everybody <u>up</u>!"

"One!"

'Happily', that never became a problem.

TWEET! TWEET! TWEET! TWEET!

"Up!"

BANG! BANG!

"Lock!"

Still, even with "The Lock" and the heat and the tar and the sweeps, I might have survived "Hell Week" unscathed if it hadn't been for one thing.

"Come on, (t)odd!"

The Prince of Marching Darkness.

"Where's The Lock, *where's* The Lock...?"

Marko-stopheles.

"Lock it! Lock it...!"

He would materialize at my side without warning, an all-too-corporeal wraith bearing irrational wrath, bettering and belittling me stride after stride:

"You call that a *lock*?"

Yes, under the watchful thighs of Marko...

"Lock, lock, lock, lock...!"

...my purgatory was complete.

But even Hell has a timeclock.

TWEEEEEEEEEET...!

"Eight A.M.! Tomorrow morning! Ready to go! Remember: To be early is to be on time; to be on time is to be late! Ba-annnd dismissed!"

This was one time Dom the Drum Major didn't have to worry about a command being followed with lightning expediency. The

Block fell out immediately – some literally – and plodded toward the gate leading back to Reveille Hall. As usual, Thor and Charlie Gupta were several steps ahead of me:

"See ya tomorrow, Will. Hey, and don't worry, it gets easier."

"Why must you lie to our boy...?"

I thought about grinning, but didn't want to expend the energy. Though I figured even if it didn't get any easier, I could at least lapse into a lock-induced coma back at the dorm and still have about 12 full hours to recover.

"(t)odd!"

Or about 12 full seconds, as it turned out.

Scene 1b: The Challenge

Remember all those players who somehow ended up below me – or more to the point, below the 75-chair cutoff – after trumpet auditions? They had all stared at me then, and I didn't understand why?

Well, I was about to find out.

Most of them had stuck around and were now staring from the grassy sideline just beyond the hard black surface of Elbert Field. They looked, well, not exactly tired since they hadn't marched all day, but... needful. I wasn't exactly sure what they needed, but they sure seemed to need it from me. Wait, not "needful"...

Hungry.

"(t)odd!"

It was Marko again. He crooked a finger and drew me to the very edge of the asphalt, grabbing one of the stray trumpets and placing him next to me. There was, in fact, an entire Noah-line being organized by the Drum Major and other Rank Leaders, instruments gathered two-by-two, one from The Block, like me, and one from the pool of desperation lapping at the sidelines.

They were called "Reserves".

They were kept on the sidelines to fill in whenever a hole appeared in The Block due to absence or illness. As incentive to endure what was essentially a thankless job, they also had the right at the end of each practice to try and earn their own place in The Block.

Which meant taking one away from somebody who already had a place. Or thought he had a place.

It was called a "Challenge".

And required each Rank Leader to put up one of his rank for potential sacrifice.

I saw Marko joking around with the Rank 9 Leader, whose own sacrificial trumpet was first in the Noah line, directly in front of me. Though the sun was almost down, there was fresh sweat on the back of this guy's neck. I recognized him as the only 3rd in a rank that was mostly 1st and 2nd trumpets. Almost as out of place as me.

And as the rest of The Block headed back to the sanctuary of Reveille Hall, laughing and belonging, I began for the very first time to get an idea of how I might have made it into Rank 8.

"First Challenge!"

At least I'd get one chance to see how it worked.

Dom the Drum Major, solemn but businesslike, led the first pair out to the nearest yardline. There was, in fact, something very gladiatorial about the whole thing, especially after Dom blew his whistle and brought the two trumpets "Up!" while a lone snare accompanied them in a side-by-side Sweep. It wasn't a race, of course, but rather a contest with three judges.

One was Dom the Drum Major, who kept his whistle in-mouthed to blow a halt to the spectacle. Another was a bearded twentysomething in faded band jacket called a "Graduate Assistant", or more commonly, "Grad Ass".

The last judge was a wild card, and depended on the particular instrument being Challenged. For this last judge was the instrument

Section Leader. The First Chair. The same for the trumpet guy now ending his Sweep as it would be for me.

Marko.

I don't remember who won or lost that First Challenge. I didn't care.

I was next.

"Second pair!"

With the first Challenge over, the Rank 9 Leader took off and Marko stopped joking around. I had his undivided attention as I stepped to the line. Except, unlike the trumpet Reserve next to me, I already knew what our Section Leader thought of my marching skills.

It was kind of like trying to skate in front of the Russian judge after an entire day of

TWEET! TWEET! TWEET! TWEET!

"Up!"

BANG! BANG!

"Lock!"

Actually, the "Up!" and "Lock!" were shouted exclusively by the Reserve, points in his favor, as the sudden onslaught of The Challenge took me by surprise. But hours of Locking had conditioned a Pavlovian knee response, and I managed to take off in step.

A "step" in marching band is not a casual distance. Length of stride is dictated by a rule known as "8-to-5". This means there are *exactly* eight steps to every five yards marched (which is not coincidentally the spacing between lines on a football field). Since a yard is 3 feet or 3 x 12 = 36 inches, and five yards is thus 5 x 36 = 180 inches, this means that each step needs to be *precisely* 180 inches divided by 8 steps = 22 ½ inches long. This is a number I could have told you even without demonstrating the math, because it was drilled into my muscular subconscious by screams of "Eight-to-five! Eight-to-five! You're not marching eight-to-five...!" And since a Challenge consisted of a 10-yard Sweep, the final math here was pretty simple:

It took only 16 steps in the fading light to strangle any small confidence I might have nurtured that day.

TWEEEEET!

BANG-BANG-BANG!

"Drop!"

I don't think I ever even saw the other guy. The Reserve.

Or the vote.

The first thing I remember coming back into focus was the face of Dom the Drum Major, speaking quietly into mine:

"You won. See you tomorrow – same time, same place, okay?"

Nodding blankly, I headed to the gate.

But I wasn't really sure where I was going anymore. The rest of the Band was way ahead of me, already crossing the street to Reveille Hall, even its tail now beyond my reach. "You won."

I was still Rank Number 82.

I had kept my address in The Block.

But as the last of the Michigan Marching Band was embraced by the warm glow of their exclusive hall, leaving me to cover the darkening distance alone, I realized that "home" was still very far away...

Scene 2: Fire Up It's Tuesday!

Duuuuuh Dut-Dut.

"Again."

That's how we spent Tuesday.

Duuuuuh Dut-Dut.

"Again."

Or at least the first couple hours of it.

Duuuuuh Dut-Dut.

"Again."

Having expended our first rehearsal inside Reveille Hall playing a single B-flat Concert tuning note, Cavendish decided to go nuts and spent our second rehearsal playing the first *three* notes of our fight song, which was written about a hundred years ago (by the dead guy Elbert Field was named after) and called "The Victors". Maybe you've heard it. The Intro starts with--

Duuuuuh Dut-Dut.

"Again."

One long, two short – a dotted half note followed by two eighths in 4/4 time or a dotted quarter followed by two sixteenths in cut time, which I point out not to brag about a working knowledge of musical time signatures (though there is that), but because you start to pay attention to the details after you've played something enough times to have it replace "be fruitful and multiply" in your brain stem. Which I believe is the subtle point Cavendish was trying to make, as he would often silently point to the sign on the side wall that said "Perfection is made up of trifles, but perfection is no trifle." Now since "The Victors" consists of roughly 433 notes in total...

Duuuuuh Dut-Dut.

"Again."

...I figured we had, roughly, 144.3 rehearsals to go to reach perfection.

Unfortunately, we had only four days to go before our first game.

Duuuuuh Dut-Dut.

"Again."

At this rate, we'd be ready to perform our *full* program...

Duuuuuh Dut-Dut.

"Again."

...about the time I graduated. Assuming, of course...

Duuuuuh Dut-Dut.

"Again."

...that I first passed Ensemble 101.

Duuuuuh Dut-Dut.

"Again."

One long, two short – the equivalent of the letter "D" in Morse Code.

Duuuuuh Dut-Dut.

"Again."

And so we spent our entire second rehearsal like some powerful voice trying to stutter out the word "D-D-Damocles" but never quite getting there – all the while waiting for the cool of the morning to burn off before heading outside to the molten tar.

Which was fine with me.

Duuuuuh Dut-Dut.

After all, I now knew what was waiting for me out there at the end of the day. A point driven home when Cavendish seemed to look directly at me after another first measure of "The Victors" was abruptly cut off:

"*Again.*"

Only the misery, as I found out, was actually going to pick up in pace...

TWEET!TWEET!TWEET!TWEET!

In marching band, there's a difference between four – very – slow – whistles and four veryfast whistles. Namely, this:

"Aggggghhhhhhhhh...!"

An "entry cadence", as it was called, begins with everyone bunched together in single file on the far sideline, making the heretofore figurative promise of a swift-kick-to-one's-ass all too literal.

In theory, you were supposed to maintain The Lock with each rapid beat. In practice, because the laws of physics occasionally overruled even the stainless steel whistle of Dom the Drum Major, you were allowed to hop and bicycle a little – but were then expected to bring your knees up even higher to balance the exertion ledger.

Another word for all this is "double-time".

However, the best word remains:

"Aggggghhhhhhhhh...!"

Even though you were supposed to anyway, you really had no choice but to scream. It was your body's way of creating a safety valve to insanity.

Physiologically, here's what's happening during an entry cadence:

Legs pump.

Lungs beg.

Sweat glands threaten to unionize.

Psychologically, it wasn't quite as complicated.

In a word:

"Aggggghhhhhhhhh...!"

Well, okay, technically, there was another word for it.

Pregame.

A lot of people think Halftime is the most important time for a marching band. They are wrong. A signature *Pregame* that drives crowd anticipation to a frenzy is the <u>true</u> hallmark of a great college band. And when you find something that works, you stick with it.

At Michigan, Pregame hadn't changed in over half a century.

It started with the following holy and inviolate incantation:

"Ladieees and Gentlemen, introducing the 275 member Meeeeechigan Marching Band: Ba-aaand, take the field!"

Followed by the aforetweeted warp-whistles:

TWEET!TWEET!TWEET!TWEET!

And pain.

"Aggggghhhhhhhhh...!"

Split in half along the far sideline, the Band would double-time it onto the field like a giant millipede scurrying across hot asphalt, keeping 500 legs in the air at a time so as not to burn its feet. Which during summer practice on Elbert Field was unfortunately more than just an analogy.

A percussion "roll-out" (the standard conclusion to any percussion cadence, a short roll followed by Digga-Digga-DUM, Digga-Digga-DUM, DUM – DUM – *DUM*) would initiate a "fan-out" to solid block "M" formation (it looked just like the capital "m" in quotes back there) so that just as everyone was about to "pass-out"...

...the show could actually begin.

"Now!"

High atop a specially built tower along the near sideline of Elbert Field, Cavendish would give a massive downbeat to the gasping Band. Under normal circumstances this would mean that everyone would start playing the "M Fanfare", our opening musical salvo. But since at this juncture we hadn't even rehearsed the music yet, the entire Michigan Marching Band did something never recommended for non-Tabernacular assemblies over 250 in count that are short on wind:

We sang.

"Daaa! *Da*-da-*da*-da-*da*-da-DAAAAA...!"

Which was fine with me.

It wasn't pretty, but it took less breath than playing, and after a Pregame entry I needed every spare molecule of air I could hoard.

In fact, I did a quick mental calculation based on the sheet music in my lyre (a miniature music stand that screws into your horn so you can read miniature pieces of music and which normally lasted about a half a season's worth of "Up!" and "Down!" before it stressed and snapped) and came up with a plan: If I panted in 2/2 time for the length of the "M Fanfare", I *just might* recover enough to undergo the next part of Pregame.

But Cavendish was apparently wise to this little scheme for self-survival, and thus he rarely ever let us "sing" entire pieces of music. Instead, he would cut us off and jump ahead to the next point of maximal physical exhaustion:

"Last note!"

"LAAAAAAAAAA...!"

For some reason, it was always "La" as in "a note to follow So" as in "So when are we going to get a chance to breathe again?".

But aspirations would have to wait.

"LOCK!"

At this point, and for the first time, we would begin marching *and* singing.

Namely, our fight song, "The Victors". At least three notes of which we could've actually played:

"Duuuuuh Dut-Dut..."

Quickly reforming into entry lines, we'd then simultaneously step off and Sweep toward the student endzone, an awesome precision Locking machine.

Right now, though, I'd like to recite a poem I composed while marching downfield.

It's called "Oxygen".

A-hem:

"Oxygen! Oxygen!

I need more oxygen!

Oh, God – oxygen!

Ox – y – geeeeen...!"

Thank you.

If then we all managed to make it to the student endzone while maintaining consciousness (this was never guaranteed), we'd use the two measure percussion break before the chorus of "The Victors" to form a traditional "floating block M" (which was, perhaps not coincidentally, a hollow version of the "solid block M"). Air would be in very short supply during those two measures down at that end of the field, and it was every lung for itself.

Panting.

Gasping.

Wheezing.

And then things got hard.

Because it was at this point that the Michigan Marching Band did something truly spectacular. Truly unexpected. Truly mind-bogglingly unnecessary.

"Arrggghhhhh...!"

We turned around *and started sweeping back upfield again.*

The way we had just come.

Without a break.

First of all, I wasn't kidding about the oxygen. Have you ever taken your body to the point that you're asking it to do something, you really *want* it to do something, you can actually *feel* your brain trying to force the command across sluggish synapses to the muscle group in question but all you're getting in reply is "Hey, I'd help you out if I could but I've already given all I can so why don't you just lay off and give us a rest before – you know what? – screw you, I quit!"?

Well, now add this voice:

"Where's The Lock? *Where's* The Lock...?"

Marko.

Back at my side.

"And I wanna hear every note! *Every* note! This is Rank 8! We play – every – note...!"

Now I couldn't have played every note if I were sitting down. And actually playing. As it was, at the edge of exhaustion, my trumpet bobbing uncontrollably in front of my face, I'd be lucky if I didn't mouthpiece an eye out.

If I had been walking, maybe, *maybe* I could have played or at least sung every note. But to sing (let alone play) every note while *Locking* was like asking me to flap my arms and fly, please. No, wait, I take that back. I actually had a better chance of flapping and winging into the air than Locking and singing every note.

But as I was to learn through the subtle interplay of mentor's voice and acolyte's ear – separated by no more than three inches and 78 decibels - this was indeed Marko's Personal Credo:

"*EVERY* – NOTE!"

So I tried through the rest of Pregame to at least hum as many of my 3rd trumpet notes as voluntary asphyxiation would allow.

Through the end of "The Victors".

Through the opposing team's fight song.

Through the "Star Spangled Banner".

Through a final chorus of "The Victors" to get us off the field and onto the sideline where we had to begin *double-timing* again.

Through a silent prayer for swift and merciful death.

And as the cadence finally concluded and a cheer arose to mark the end of our first Pregame drill, an answer to my prayer came from on high:

"Again!"

Cavendish.

Shouting down from his sideline tower.

I looked heavenward to see him backlit by the still ascending sun while the rest of the Band scrambled back across the tar to start all over again. It was the answer to my prayer, all right.

Except for the "swift and merciful" part...

By the end of the day, with the sun taking a bow by mooning me on the horizon and the rest of the Band heading home, as I was inevitably put up as the inevitable Rank 8 representative for the inevitable Challenge, I thought about committing Block Suicide. I could end this right here, right now.

TWEET! TWEET! TWEET! TWEET!

"Up!"

BANG! BANG!

"Lock!"

But sometimes nature conspires against you. Today's Reserve was God's Gift to Incoordination. He looked like he was marching to an AA meeting.

"And DROP!"

The judges didn't take long. I think even Marko had to vote for me. Though the look on his face held no sanction, so I turned and limped back to the gate. It didn't matter anyways.

I had won the Challenge.

I'd be back again tomorrow.

To do it all over again.

Scene 3: Fire Up It's Wednesday!

It's come time for an ugly confession.

I put it off as long as possible, but really can't anymore.

You see, this is a period piece. I went to college years ago, but have been trying to make my story as non-specific as possible so that you the reader could find something universal in it. And just like you can ignore the fact that this story takes place at the University of Michigan if that bugs you, if the time period I'm about to identify seems too old, or not old enough, you can pretty much ignore that, too. It really doesn't matter for the important stuff to follow. However, in keeping with my promise to adhere as close as possible to The Truth, well...

It's come time for an ugly confession.

The next morning inside Reveille Hall, we actually began rehearsing our halftime music. Now unlike most marching bands, we had our own in-house arranger, a graduate student whose name, perhaps appropriately, was John. This meant that instead of having to play standard catalogue music that was at best a year or two behind the times and at worst a decade or two... or more ("Give My Regards to Broadway", "Hooray For Hollywood", and Satan's own "Strike Up The Band") or *way* more (principally any sound Sousa ever produced, including, I think, bodily functions), we in the MMB could play *contemporary* music while it was still more or less contempored.

Of course, just because you *have* the power to do something doesn't mean you should.

Because having our own in-house arranger meant that John had been busy all summer painting with the sophisticated musical palette available to him – brass and percussion – to transpose into march-ready compositions the music of the moment. The genre of a generation. This further meant that when Cavendish finally threw us his most definitive downbeat that morning, the brass, led, as usual, by the 75-member trumpet section, took its deepest collective breath and unleashed an incomparable, indefensible, brain-pan rattling quadruple-fortissimo

AH – AH – AH – AH...!

inflamed and bloated and swelling to burst by a crescendoing roll from an entire rank-and-a-half of bicep-popping percussionists who finally exploded in head-flagellating syncopation while the rest of the Band climaxed full force in an absolutely blood-curdling

STAYIN' ALI I I I I I I I I I I I I I I I I I I I I I I I I I I I I I I I I I I I I I I I I I IVE!

which belied the ignominious death that was soon to come.

Though not soon enough, and so the ugly confession:

We played Disco.

Marching Band Style.

I weep for my generation.

Fortunately, the morning also delivered something far more fashionable...

Uniforms.

Since I was still in The Block, I got the full workup: Hat, gloves, cords, spats...

Okay, maybe "fashionable" wasn't the right word.

I know there's a certain militant goofiness to marching band uniforms, and ours was no exception. But as I stood in the locker area with everyone else admiring newly assigned components, trying them on one by one, cloaking my formless freshman novitiate self with the sacramental (and field-tested) raiment, slowly becoming indistinguishable from those around me, I actually began to feel – momentarily, but I'd take it – like I *almost-belonged.*

One thing's for sure, when you rammed home that 18-inch feathered plume into the top of your hat and stood up straight and looked at yourself in a mirror, you not only felt like you were 7 feet tall...

You <u>were</u> 7 feet tall.

Even The Lock felt better when protected by the heavy canvas of the pant leg. And as I held it in the mirror, I realized that if I ignored myself from the neck up, I now made a fair approximation to the recruiting poster I'd seen at Registration.

I had literally added a dimension to what had once seemed a flat, distant dream.

And at that moment, like a dream, I thought I could feel things begin to turn around. Today was Wednesday, "Hump Day", and perhaps not coincidentally "Hump!" was also a term veteran band members used as a vocal punctuation to conclude certain difficult tasks. Maybe this was my "Hump!" day, then, too.

Maybe I had crested the hardest part of the week.

Maybe, within this unbaptized uniform, I had witnessed the peak...

"Jive!"

Back out on Elbert Field, practice actually seemed to be getting easier. Our Halftime program wasn't nearly as life-threatening as Pregame, and started with a horns-down sensibly-tempoed entry from the four corners of the field while "hand-jiving" in precise unison – two strokes palm down, two strokes palm up – accompanied by a drum cadence syncopated for maximal funkiness.

It was, in fact, a textbook Marching Band Disco Entry.

Sillier. But easier.

Charlie and Thor even found time for chit-chat:

"I am wondering quite frankly if people will even recall this thing called Rock-N-Roll in ten years time from now."

"What are you babbling about, Charlie?"

"Hey, be facing reality, please – Disco is most certainly here to stay."

Charlie, by the way, was an economics major.

Thor looked back over his shoulder and gave me a grin which, incredibly, I had enough energy to return. It almost caused me to miss my next Lock as I realized I had just experienced a second moment of almost-belonging. In one day.

In Rank 8.

I felt my hand-jives intensi-funk.

Nobody was passing judgement on me right now. Even better, hours later, near the end of practice, I actually got to sit down, relax...

...and pass judgement on *others* for a change.

TWEEEEET!

"Double command! Ten-hut! Ten-hut! One, two, three!"

Hmm, a little rushed.

The occasion was Drum Major tryouts. Three guys vying for the-right-hand-of-God spot in the Michigan Marching Band. While the rest of us sat on the cool grass of the sidelines, they toed an imaginary line on the asphalt, each yelling and then executing a series of commands. The first was "Attention" done as a "double command", which was the standard way of doing it, meaning that instead of freezing each step "by the numbers", the command was executed in tempo to the Drum Major's yell.

The first guy had definitely rushed a little.

Dom was up next. And even though he had already held the job for the past two years and was a virtual shoo-in for a third, he still had to go through the motions in front of the entire Band:

TWEEEEEEEEEET!

"Double command! Ten - hut! Ten - hut! One! Two! Three!"

Three perfect Locks. We weren't supposed to be partial, but:

"Ooooooo..."

Yet the one that really got to me was the last guy.

FWOOO...! FWOOO...!

Something about this guy's whistle wasn't quite right. I think he might have been using a duck call by mistake.

"Dupple commaaaaand!"

He was slight and prematurely balding, and had some kind of odd, modulating... trans-Anglo accent.

"A-teeen-shut! A-teeen-shut! Uh-One...! Uh-Two...! Uh-Three...!"

Holding each Lock a hair too long, feet flat, it now seemed possible that his whistle might have been a duck call after all.

A chain reaction of snickers swept through the Band, and seeing an opportunity for the day's third almost-belonging moment, I joined in.

The Truth is, it was hard not to.

He just stood there with his out-sized non-regulation baton in stiff, Grenadierian attention, ignoring the smirks.

And even before the inevitable overwhelming vote for Dom--

"Yeaaaaaaaaaaa...!"

--I no longer felt like the Band's biggest loser.

But the best part of it was...

...I was able to carry that feeling into my next Challenge.

"And – <u>drop</u>!"

And you know what happened?

As I stood at Attention with yet another heavy-breathing trumpet Reserve beside me, I saw Dom conferring with the other judges. The Grad Ass.

And Marko.

I then saw Dom stepping over to us with a look of sympathy on his face.

And I heard him say

“I’m sorry...”

before he looked right at me and continued

“Good job, Will. See you tomorrow.”

I had won.

Now, I’ll bet a lot of you thought there was going to be a typical story-telling reversal there and I was going to lose. Admit it. Well, The Truth is, a little confidence is the best weapon you can carry into a challenge.

And this time, when it was all over, I didn’t trudge to the gate. I *ran* to catch up with the rest of the Band.

Hump!

In just one practice, I had gone from fearing yesterday, to actually looking forward to...

Scene 4: Fire Up It's Thursday!

So while I'm in a good mood, let's try a digression.

The topic is "Girls."

Here we go:

Band had 'em.

I didn't.

End of digression.

Scene 4a: Fire Up It's Girls!

Actually, it's not quite that simple.

It never is.

And since every story is required by law to have some sort of romance – no matter how manufactured...

SLAM!

That was my locker. Just across from the "Girls" restroom. I used to slam it a lot after seeing a particularly good-looking (or for that matter, at that age, even particularly proximate) female Band member come or go, symbolizing all-too clearly a place I was seemingly forever forbidden.

Meaning "Girls", not the bathroom.

Let's start with some basic facts.

There was a time not too long ago when marching bands didn't allow any girls at all. But this was the enlightened age of Disco, filled with Farrah-clones and fully-contoured "Afternoon Delight" T-shirts. The locker hall was filled with them, and for me, proof enough of the wisdom of our shorts-only rehearsal policy.

Like the MMB itself, the MMB locker hall was co-ed, and even more co-ed than most because we believed in something many other marching bands didn't. And believe me, I'm more disappointed than you to report that that something was not "Free Love".

It was called "Blend".

See, the prime directive of most marching bands is to be... well, all you had to do was go from locker hall to rehearsal hall during warm-ups to have the perfect word come immediately to mind, drilled, in fact, straight into your forebrain. And that word would be:

"Ow."

As in, "Ow, my ears hurt." Or, if you're looking strictly for an adjective, that adjective would be "LOUD". As in:

"OW, MY EARS HURT!"

Now "loud" means predominantly "brass" and "brass" means predominantly "male". For even in this enlightened age, there was a distinct segregation of the sexes by instrument.

For instance, take the percussion section – please! (rimshot) (a multi-goon stick-denting mega-rimshot) – virtually all male. There was one cymbal player who was a girl, but she was a Reserve and so didn't really count and besides, it was rumored she might have a Y-chromosome or two floating around in her genome.

So where did all the (Band) Girls come from?

Well, since the MMB preferred a more "orchestral" sound - or "blend" - we also recruited a number of softer, or "fairer", instruments.

Here they are by section:

Piccolos. The reigning rank of femininity. "Woe to any man with a fife, for he shall be outcasteth amongst his brethren." 100% female.

Clarinets. Another of the womanly woodwind family, with a few mama's boys thrown in for good measure. 90% female.

Sax. Like it's near-homophone, not an instrument with which I had much familiarity. I'd estimate less than 50% female.

As for my own highly masculine instrument, we in the trumpet section did get the occasional valve-crasher. These came in two varieties:

The Butch and The Beautiful.

Out of 75 total chairs, we had exactly one of each.

The Butch had a fondness for warming up with the theme from "Rocky". Between her and Bela Abzug, Bela had the better shot at a Revlon contract. Especially if it were scored on looks *and* personality. The poor guy who sat next to her during rehearsals in Reveille Hall developed "Pisa Syndrome" after a season of listing to leeward.

Fortunately, the Butch was far removed in the 1st trumpets, where she had something to prove. *Un*fortunately, the Beautiful was also far removed, in the 2nd trumpets...

...where she had nothing more she *could* prove. In an era before health clubs, she was a darkly tanned, deeply toned girl with long straight brown hair and two "this better be good" eyes – and a body that would have made Conan the Barbarian want to throw on a T-shirt.

She sat right on the end of a row directly opposite the tuning machine, a little brown box that electronically checked the frequency of your B-flat Concert and was almost always ignored but now generated the most devoted line in marching band. The most polite, too, as you'd have a clear view of the Beautiful all the way up to the box ("Hey, take your time there." "After you." "No rush." "Tut, tut, I insist...") Her legs were right out of a Marvel comic. And God knows what she could do with that embouchure.

All in all, it made for a very well-tuned ensemble.

But the real lottery winner wasn't the guy who got to sit beside her all season in Reveille Hall...

...but the guy who got to march *behind* her all season on Elbert Field.

He was a perpetually overheated 2nd trumpet who never had a problem keeping his eyes glued forward during Attention.

But who did, occasionally, give new meaning to "The Lock":

TWEET! TWEET! TWEET! TWEET!

"Up!"

BANG! BANG!

"*Nnn*ggh!"

He didn't seem to mind the pain.

TWEEEEET!

"At ease..."

But as far as I was concerned, there was really only one section in the marching band for girls.

They practiced slightly apart from the rest of The Block, by themselves.

They were distant...

Exotic.

An entire corps of healthy young women from the heartland who either didn't play an instrument or couldn't get into The Block with the one they did play.

And hence had been deepened by a tragic element.

They filled two full ranks at the very front of the Band, and from my disad-vantage point embedded in the middle of The Block it was often difficult to see them. That is, until they crouched down and snapped up their definitive emblems.

They were mysterious.

They had secrets.

They had...

SNAP!

Flags.

But there was one flag in particular that stood apart.

She was the most perfect girl in the entire corps.

The flag de la flag...

Jeannie Winterspoon.

She was Grace Kelly in marching shorts. A princess who had somehow gotten lost in the Midwest on the way to her coming-out ball. She was...

Totally unobtainable.

Jeannie Winterspoon was more than just eight ranks away. She was like a star whose light could only be perceived across vast, silent expanses of time. A celestial body...

With *great* legs.

The question was, how could a boy like me defy the laws of physics and approach this celestial body radiating such great light – and heat – without getting burned?

"Water!"

Wishing to avoid (further) incidences of prostration, the Band had taken to setting up water coolers on chairs along the near sideline, and (reluctantly) calling for frequent rehydration breaks. There were plastic trash cans at each station, and a supply of paper cups.

Of such slight materials are moments of destiny built:

"Oh! Pardon me..."

Worlds – and our cups – had collided on their way to the spigot.

Her voice had been exactly what you would have expected, a bell reverberating from a steeple, reminiscent more of song than speech, vespers than voice.

I steadied my own before replying, somewhat over-gallantly, but this was no time to veil Arthurian intentions:

"No, no – please..."

And what was this? A glimpse beneath her unassailable surface to a slight imperfection that made her all the more perfect with – could it be? – a hint of shyness?

"Oh, I couldn't..."

That was it. I went for it.

"But you must."

We both knew it was a goofy thing to say. A *gloriously* goofy thing, for she smiled as she replied with a simple but oh-so-sincere

"Thank you."

She placed her cup under the spigot.

But it was I who reached for the stars:

"Allow me."

Our hands met at the tap. And, then, finally, our eyes. And the dribbling water swelled like music, as nature itself consecrated our epidermal union.

About the only thing missing was the theme from "Romeo and Juliet"...

...and any semblance to The Truth.

Let's face it: With a girl like Jeannie Winterspoon, there was only one way this could turn out.

"Water!"

Now, cups could indeed collide.

"Oh, I'm sorry."

"No, no – it's okay."

And eyes could indeed meet.

And even hold.

Until:

"I have a boyfriend on the football team."

Which, of course, isn't true, either.

I just felt I had to give you a couple of story extremes to bound a reality you might not like:

"Water!"

An incidental collision of cups, followed by a not particularly interested

"Oh..."

No need for me to say a word, just motion her to continue filling her cup...

...and watch her walk away.

That was it. Nothing more. And you know what?

Even <u>that's</u> an exaggeration.

"Water!"

The Truth is the boy never even got close to Jeannie Winterspoon. Never even heard the sound of her voice.

Never even tried...

I was often one of the first people back out on the field after a water break, toeing the line while others drank more fully, and now finally able to see the dual rows of flags so many ranks ahead but lying unfurled on the dark surface of the asphalt while their guardians sought contact beyond their own kind in greener sidelines. I watched it all from my place. From the stickiness of the tar. Through the near empty Block.

From afar.

So much for "Girls".

Now some of you may be wondering why the heck I brought this up in the first place if nothing happened. "Damn depressing, Stud." Yeah, well...

...something did happen. But not for a long time.

I promise I'll tie it all in when we get to the end of the story.

But for now...

...I had other Challenges to face.

TWEET! TWEET! TWEET! TWEET!

"Up!"

Another Reserve. Another 10-yard Sweep. My fourth in as many days.

But the day had gone pretty well again, and I was beginning to think that maybe, just maybe – someday – there just might be...

BANG! BANG!

"Lock!"

...a band jacket in the future with my name on it.

Now nobody would've been caught dead wearing a band jacket in high school (I still have mine, fresh as the day it came off the lame, er, loom). (Actually, that was a lie. True, I still have my high school band jacket, but I always kind of liked it, and regret never having worn it while I could...)

But here it was different.

MMB jackets were forged of substantial cloth and bright piping and years of devotion, and besides the requisite letter sewn over your heart, were embellished with circular patches down the length of one sleeve no more than three inches in diameter, but each a testament to a special journey made out-of-state at the end of marching season, medals of honor worn only by Veterans of Foreign Bowls. The jackets were further personalized with embroidery. Your instrument...

And your name:

Todd

Trumpet

It had a nice ring to it.

All the Grad Asses wore them. Even in the heat. This included the Grad Ass judge who followed me and my fourth Reserve (in as many days) during our 10-yard Challenge. The Reserve didn't seem to care, but the jacket was like a siren song to me, calling and luring to faraway locales. The Grad Ass had four patches, each individually designed, one orange and three roses, one Florida and three Californias...

Who knew what exotic lands would grace my own sleeve someday? It filled me with a feeling of...

Digga-Digga-DUM, Digga-Digga-DUM, DUM – DUM – *DUM*!

Pride.

"And – drop!"

And that's when I missed the yardline.

The worst possible yardline to miss, the last one at the end of the Sweep where you drop your horn and come to Attention. No room to fudge your 8-to-5. Arches squarely on the white line. No place to hide.

And so, seeing the Reserve at my side and wondering why he was a little behind me, I glanced down at my feet.

I had over-stepped the line.

Now I know what you're thinking. "Pride goeth before a fall." The ol' hubris thing, right? You're expecting another one of those story reversals where just when you thought I was getting the hang of this stuff, I lose, aren't you? Well...

"It wasn't unanimous, but..."

...you're right.

Dom the Drum Major was looking at the Reserve now. And from the side of the field, so was the Grad Ass. Somewhat sheepishly. Like he was trying to avoid looking directly at me. But not the third judge.

And not sheepish at all. While Dom delivered the verdict to the Reserve...

Marko had eyes only for me.

"You take over Block Number 82. Report directly to your Rank Leader. Will... I'm sorry."

And that was it.

That's what really happened.

I lost The Challenge.

I lost my position in The Block.

I lost my place in Band.

But it wasn't until...

Scene 5: Fire Up It's Friday!

...that I realized just how much I had lost.

Friday was the day the entire Band had been looking forward to – the day we rehearsed beyond the white-washed confines of Reveille Hall, beyond the black-tarred familiarity of Elbert Field, to the living-colored sacristy of...

(Hush)

Michigan Stadium.

(Hush)

The largest college football crucible in the world.

(Un-hush)

Though I had grown up watching the games on TV, I had never actually stepped inside Michigan Stadium before. Now, on the threshold of that moment, standing in the stadium parking lot with the rest of The Block – in the very last (non)rank – I came not as one of the anointed, but as one of the

"Reserves!"

The Grad Ass waved us forward, finally submitting to the heat of the hottest summer on record by abandoning his band jacket to a pile of wooden crates outside the entrance tunnel. Yes, we would get to go inside first, not carrying our chosen instruments or what remained of our pride, but podiums, stands, and any other equipment that might be needed to support the *real* Band.

Me, I shouldered a long wooden ladder, and as I dragged it rank-by-rank past the immobile Block, I felt like I was walking the Via Dolorosa, except that instead of being stoned I was being stone-walled – some in the Band even turning away to avert their eyes.

I had become a leper, one of the untouchables.

An outcast.

I quickened my pace, trying to outrun the feeling clamping down around my chest, and Michigan Stadium loomed larger and larger – all the more gargantuan and ominous for a knowledge that most of it actually lay unseen, below the surface, dug into the earth like a giant bowl.

Or a giant grave.

Or perhaps an iceberg would be most appropriate, for unbeknownst to me then, while soon to be afloat at its periphery, I was to experience a Titanic moment in my young life.

But first the tunnel, long and dark and emerging into a vastly unexpected space, 100,000 empty seats, not at all like I had perceived it would be or had ever seen it before, absent of the humanity that on a given Saturday would make this yawing chasm the fifth biggest city in the state, not a silent bowl but a giant bell trumpeting heavenward a voice that even when hushed would pulse with a life force that was now unnaturally absent. It felt...

Mute.

Or maybe it was because *I* felt mute.

Or maybe it was because I was schlepping a damn ladder.

One thing's for sure:

"Reserves! Don't go *on* the field, go *around* it!"

This didn't help. It was now apparent that the storied carpet of Michigan Stadium was not to be defiled by the foot of a Reserve. I was to be denied even that. And by a jacketless Grad Ass.

I squinted into the punishing sun. The sky may have been clear--

"Reserves! *All* Reserves...!"

--but a storm was brewing nevertheless.

"Get out of the way!"

And then the thunder exploded.

TWEETTWEETTWEETTWEET!

BANGBANGBANGBANG!

"YAHHHHHHHHHH...!"

A thunderstorm of voices – about 999,725 short of capacity but enough to turn the tunnel into a soul-splitting stadium horn – blew down the length of the 50-yard line to cleanse the sins of off-season and clear a path onto which Pregame Entry could burst forth. And forth they burst, two by two, double-timing with arms raised like True Believers led back to the Promised Land...

...while I watched from the sideline.

Mute.

The Band blurring past me.

They took possession of the field like they owned it.

Like they belonged.

Band blurring past...

But that way was lost to me. And couldn't be recovered. Challenges wouldn't be allowed again until Monday. Not that it mattered. You only get to enter Michigan Stadium for the first time in your life *once*.

Band blurring...

And so I turned my back, leaning my burden against a wall, coming face to face with a small stenciled sign. It read, unambiguously, in plain white English:

"P l a y e r s O n l y".

"Reserves!"

So instead of marching, I listened to a jacketless Grad Ass instruct us on how we'd spend our Saturday – tomorrow – Game Day – steadying ladders, hauling equipment, and most especially upholding a long-standing tradition of--

"Apples – go!"

--fetching boxes of fruit at Halftime for the nourishment of the worthy.

The guy actually had a stopwatch, and he and I both stood stock still as the entire Reserve corps (go ahead and pronounce it like it's spelled) scurried back into the tunnel for a time trial while the Band swept out over the forbidden field, playing, of all things, "The Victors". Finally, the jacketless Grad Ass looked up from his timepiece and gave me a glance as if to ask, "Well?"

Well, indeed.

And so I made a decision.

I hustled back into the tunnel, past Reserves already re-emerging with empty apple boxes carried between them, past more crates waiting to be transported...

And I kept on running.

Right through to the other side, beyond the portal to Michigan Stadium, beyond the Band, The Block, Reserves, Rank 8, and Chair #74.

Back out to the vacant parking lot.

Back out to Everyday.

Which is where I paused.

I know it may not seem like much to you sitting there – a kid about to quit band, so what?

But there are times in your life when you realize that no matter how mundane the decision is you're about to make, it's going to color everything you do from that point forward.

I was at that point. Just staring ahead, breathing hard, looking out and in for anything anything that could provide an answer. This really was one of the hardest decisions I ever had to make. The Big Quit. And you know what tipped the scales? Get ready, because this is getting close to an actual storybook moment here...

The goddamn band jacket.

That's right. The one the Grad Ass had left on a stack of apple crates just outside the tunnel entrance. I saw it out of the corner of my eye, and the damn patches that went with it. This stupid little... *trivial* piece of... wool was actually giving me pause. Wool! In the dead heat of summer, the last possible *worst* material you would want to wear right now. Meant for conditions that were hard to even *imagine* right now. Fall and Winter and cold and exams and new years and...

How could you even look ahead that far?

And those stupid little patches. And the embroidery with your instrument. And your name... Though you had to admit, they did a nice job with the stitching. I ran my fingers over it. Real solid. In fact, the whole garment had a certain solid heft to it. Weighty. Substantial...

Trivial!

I dunno. Or was it? Is anything that helps you make a decision like this trivial? I really don't know. All I know is--

"Ungh...!"

--I picked up an apple box and, straining under the weight, headed back into the darkened tunnel.

Even though I couldn't see any light at the end...

Act Three: Game Day

Scene 1: Fire Up It's Saturday!

I'd like to say things immediately improved after I made that momentous decision--

"Reserve!"

--but they didn't.

Early Saturday morning.

The Band started out on Elbert Field for their final practice before the game, which wouldn't start for hours. They called this a "dress rehearsal" because in addition to standard shorts and T-shirts (didn't want to sweat up the uniforms), everyone had to wear their band hats, 18-inch plume and all--

"Reserve!"

--even Reserves, who were honored with the task of policing the asphalt for litter before the start of practice so nobody who was actually going to high step in today's game would have to navigate around a gum wrapper.

In fact, Reserves were subject to a number of unique humiliations on Game Day, though so far, I had been spared the--

"Will!"

--worst. Great. The Grad Ass knew my name.

He was standing on the sideline with a cute piccolo player with a bent plume. I could tell what was coming, but there was no way to avoid it. Like drones in a hive, a Reserve's only mandate was to serve The Block. I marched to my fate.

And so, without preamble, on the morning of my first big day at college, the Grad Ass reached above my head, took a firm grip, yanked hard and--

FWOOM!

I was deplumed.

“Carry on.”

Yeah. More like “carrion”. Except even dead rotting carcasses don’t have to go back on litter patrol. A full foot and a half shorter than anybody else.

I had now hit the *literal* low point of MMB.

“Will...!”

What? What did they want from me now? A *kidney*?

I looked up to see Dom the Drum Major beckoning me to midfield. But even with his own 30-inch yeti-like hat and plume, I barely noticed him. For standing at his side was someone whose scalpel-like glare seemed to have in mind a target distinctly south of my kidneys.

It was Marko.

And I had never seen him look so angry. I didn’t know what was going on – heck, I had already been booted from Rank 8, Trumpet Valhalla, what more could they do? But from the look on Marko’s face, I saw it would take the intervention of no less than Odin himself to pull me out of this one.

“Hey, did you hear about Thor’s father...?”

Two trumpets, passing by. What the heck were they...?

“(t)odd!”

I double-timed it over to my former Rank Leader, but it was Dom who did the talking:

"Will, listen – Thor's dad had a heart attack."

Now, just so this doesn't turn tragic, I'll use the mandatory respectful pause here to let you know that Thor's dad recovered fully. Then it was my turn to say something:

"He did?"

"Last night. We need you to march in his spot – 81."

Marko was next, under his breath – seething:

"There are more *senior* Reserves."

"He marched right next to his position for almost the entire week, now lay off, Marko."

It was the first time I'd ever heard Dom raise his voice without a preparatory whistle. But one thing was clear nonetheless.

This was a command.

In response, Marko threw his hands into a biblical resignation that would have embarrassed Cecile B. DeMille.

I prepared for hard bondage.

But Marko just silently cursed a commandment or two and stormed away.

Leaving me with Dom. And a sense that maybe someone had taken notice of my Hell Week plight after all.

"Come on, Will..."

And so, just like that, I was back in The Block. I was going to march on Game Day after all. I was going to march in Michigan Stadium in front of 100,000 screaming fans...

"Right here."

...right – next – to Marko.

It's true. Dom led me straight to Thor's position, Block Number 81. Right next to my old position, 82, now occupied by the trumpet Reserve who had beat me two days ago in a Challenge.

And at the head of the rank, directly to my right, less than a yardlength away with no intervening humanity, Block Number 80, eight-zero – *ground* zero of Rank 8 – and he was armed and ready to blow. The second I touched the yardline, he abandoned it, scowling and prowling and laying down the law:

"All right, Rank 8, *listen up*!"

We listened up.

"This is Saturday. Game Day. *No excuses day*. There are only three things you need to remember today. One: You will Lock on every step! *Every* step! I had better not have to ask even one person, *one person* 'Where's The Lock?' today – this is Game Day – we Lock on every step! And on every step you will play every note! That's *Two*: *Every* note! This is Rank 8! *My* rank! I play every note – *you* will play every note! Every – note!"

To have added my name would have been sort of superfluous, as Marko was now standing right in front of me looking right at me, as he had been for most of this pep talk.

But Dom was still by my side, and countered in a lower voice:

"Don't worry about playing the notes. Just concentrate on learning the new position, okay?"

With Marko still searing away most of the life force in my immediate vicinity, I couldn't quite get my head to nod. But Dom had done all he could, and left me with a pat on the back that only served to intensify Marko's visual vivisection.

Of course, he wasn't quite finished. Until someone at a safe distance finally gave him his cue:

"Hey, Marko, what about Three?"

"Three..."

But the rest of the rank would have to guess about Three, because I was the only one who heard it, close to my ear, practically whispered.

Or hissed:

"...I'll be watching."

Kickoff was at 12:00.

High Noon.

Like it or not, I was back in the game...

Scene 2: Rituals

I was also back in full uniform as--

TWACK!

--Dom himself rammed home a fresh straight plume into my hat.

Uniform inspection took place in front of Reveille Hall, with the entire Block standing compressed between the steps and the street, each member individually scrutinized by Drum Major and Rank Leader.

Dom himself was easy to spot, trussed up in a pure white head-to-toe equestrian superhero uniform with enough piping to outfit every usher in the state. But I wouldn't have cared if he had been wearing tassels – come to think of it, there probably were some on his boots – but who cared? – I was wearing white gloves myself, everybody was, everybody else in The Block, everybody else in the MMB, everybody else--

In the Band.

Where the Drum Major himself was now squaring me up by the shoulders, nodding his approval, *smiling* his approval before moving on down the line. And as I stood for a time at Attention, I became slowly aware that he had left me with more than just a new plume...

I was grinning.

Now, in Truth, with kickoff less than an hour away, inspection was really just a show for the crowds on the way to the stadium. Nobody ever got booted during inspection. Of course, I didn't know that. To me, I had just passed an important test, proving that I could stand with the rest of the Band.

Besides, I was actually starting to enjoy myself, from my fresh straight plume right down to my--

"Dirty wrinkled spats."

Spats were those flaps of anachronistic leather snap-buttoned around the shoe that were meant to be kept blindingly white at all times, the better to see each raised footstep, and were last in vogue around, well, the time white gloves were in vogue, both surviving into the modern era principally because of weddings, funerals, and marching bands. Of the three, from where I now stood, with Marko taking his inspection stance directly in front of me, I was already ruling out weddings or marching bands...

"You were told to polish those. Did you?"

"Uhhh, well... they're... well... they're brand new."

"That's not what I asked."

His hand suddenly shot out – I think he just wanted to see me flinch – check – and then pulled my mouthpiece. He leered inside, and from his expression, you would have thought Marko was taking his first peek into a sphincter-scope:

"You put this in your *mouth*?"

"I... used a pipe cleaner to--"

"That's not what I asked."

He replaced the mouthpiece in the neck of my trumpet, giving it the kind of sharp and sudden twist that farmer's use when they don't want to dirty an axe.

"Don't worry. You'll have plenty of time to clean everything up again – come Monday."

His meaning was clear. And he had a point. Thor probably would be back on Monday, and I'd be back on the sidelines, on the outside looking in, waiting for my one chance each day to Challenge back into The Block.

I wouldn't belong for long...

"I have a better idea."

It was Dom, who had been inspecting the rank behind us, but now stepped up again to face me.

And an amused Marko:

"<u>Do</u> you, Dom?"

"Yeah, I do. *Marko*."

I couldn't help but add my own "Yeah, *Marko*".

Silently, of course.

Though Dom soon offered an opportunity to use it aloud, turning back to me:

"You were Challenged four days in a row this week, weren't you, Will?"

"Yeah..."

I decided to save the "*Marko*" for later. Like when I wrote this book.

Dom then glanced at the Reserve in my former spot.

And back again to Marko:

"And after Thor gets back, there'll be more Challenges for this exact same spot, won't there?"

"So?"

“So what if we treat today like the Ultimate Challenge – not just 10 yards on Elbert Field but a whole *game* in Michigan Stadium – and whoever performs best gets to *keep* this spot for an entire week, no, two weeks, until our next home game – no other Challenges allowed.”

“That’s not the rules.”

“That’s not what I asked.”

It was at this moment that I realized “Dom” was short for “Domini” as in “Anno Domini” as in how else to explain that Marko suppressed an entirely obvious urge to tear the three foot head and hat from the Drum Major’s shoulders and affix it to his baton and instead merely simmered in homicidal silence?

“Then it’s settled. Guys...”

Dom turned to me and the Reserve - though to my mind, mostly me:

“...good luck.”

He then returned to the rank behind us to continue inspection and fight crime and bring light and warmth to the hearts of good children everywhere.

Marko didn’t see it that way.

In fact, it was a miracle – or another – that he could see at all, as his eyes seemed about ready to explode and take out a substantial portion of the mid-Block and any other innocent stadium-goers who had the bad luck to be within 30 feet of me and therefore in range of his deadly optic shrapnel.

But for the second time that minute he suppressed an urge to kill and instead turned his attention to the Reserve:

"Listen, don't sweat it. I'm still one of the judges..."

Actually, he wasn't talking for the benefit of the Reserve at all.

"...and I'm sure *you'll* do fine."

Marko moved past me like I was already gone, continuing his inspection down the rank.

There was nothing left to do but wait. And stand at Attention. And think about the chance to get my spot back in The Block. So I made a minor adjustment to my horn carry. Why? Because if it was going to be me against the Reserve in a Game Day side-by-side Ultimate Challenge, I was going to give it my ultimate best.

151% effort.

And I would out-attention this guy during inspection...

And I would out-parade this guy on the way to the stadium...

And I would out-tunnel this guy in the last few minutes before Pregame.

"Let's go Blue! Let's go Blue...!"

Our school colors were yellow and blue.

"Let's go Blue! Let's go Blue...!"

If you don't like yellow and blue, you can think of two other colors, but I'm going to need them for what's coming up.

"Let's go Blue! Let's go Blue...!"

Blue was our symbol of unity and strength.

Blue was the very fabric of our uniform.

Even the word itself could be used as a shout of exultation, but more often was chanted as a three-beat full-fisted invocation:

"Let's go Blue! Let's go Blue...!"

It was the Band chanting it right now. All 275 of us, at the top of our lungs, packed chest-to-back in entry lines like firecrackers waiting for a light.

But the light seemed still distant from where I stood, engulfed by the darkness of the tunnel, the noise of the gathering crowd beyond more felt than heard – unlike the sound of the Reserve behind me shouting into my ear, or my own voice tearing to find a higher harmonic:

"Let's go Blue...!"

"LET'S GO BLUE...!"

The football team added their own pre-evolutionary yelps on the way back to the locker room, clearing the field for Pregame – when someone threw a switch and the tunnel suddenly fell silent, wedging the last--

"LET'S GUH—"

--in my throat. The opposing team had entered the tunnel. And now passed in close quarters to 275 souls who refused to look at them.

A single foreign jersey tried to raise an inspirational whoop, but it died without echo along this block of discipline.

As psyche-outs go, it was a pretty good one.

And as I stood there, pressed on all sides by The Block and the silence and the darkness and the Ultimate Challenge that was now moments away, I began to wonder if maybe *I* wasn't being psyched out, too.

The tunnel was beginning to clear, leaving us alone for the first time. And so the Band began its final Pregame tunnel tradition, the singing of our alma mater, "The Yellow and Blue".

Not knowing the words, I could only stand and listen.

And reflect.

"Sing to the colors,

That float in the light;

Hurrah for The Yellow and Blue."

I began to wonder what was really happening here.

"Yellow the stars,

As they ride through the night;

And reel in a rollicking crew."

What was really important?

"Yellow the fields,

Where ripens the grain..."

Maybe I'd been wrong about this whole thing.

"And yellow the moon,

On the harvest wane – *Hail*!"

Maybe I'd been underselling myself this whole time.

"Hail to the colors,

That float in the light..."

And maybe the question I really needed to ask was--

"<u>Hurrah</u> for The Yellow and Blue!"

Was I Yellow...?

"LET'S GO BLUE! LET'S GO BLUE...!"

...or was I Blue?

TWEEEEEEEEEET!

"Ladieeeees and Gentlemen! *In*troducing the 275 member Mmmmmichigan Marching Band!"

Amplified.

A distant voice.

About to light the fuse.

"BA-AAAAAAAAAAND...!"

Scene 3: Entry

"...TAKE THE FIELD!!!"

And it was only in that moment, finally seeing the light at the end of the tunnel...

TWEET! TWEET! TWEET! TWEET!

"Hup!"

BANG! BANG!

"Lock!"

...that I knew what to do.

"YAHHHHHHHHHH...!"

Instead of the expected – as the tunnel shattered in Entry Cadence and The Block screamed and surged toward the light and I finally came upon the door to the living...

"WAHHHHHHHHHHHHHHHHHHHHHHHHHH...!"

...I chose to be reborn.

I can't even tell you what it's like to enter Michigan Stadium on a Game Day Saturday in front of God, country, and a tenth of a million screaming fans.

I can't tell you because I really didn't notice. I was intent on just one thing. And it wasn't the trumpet Reserve literally nipping at my heels in one of the frequent bunch-ups that occurred during double-time entry onto the field.

No.

Instead, I had decided to face the *ultimate* Ultimate Challenge of the Michigan Marching Band.

Right in front of me. Like it had always been. Like it would always *be*.

Right there. Right in my way.

Right in front of my eyes...

Marko.

And if he was the best the MMB had to offer, I would match him step for step...

“Ahhhhhhhhhh...!”

“AHHHHHHHHHH...!”

...and note for note.

The scream I unleashed startled even me, and Marko actually gave a half-glance over his shoulder to make sure something hadn’t been killed behind him.

But in a way, something had been killed.

And if he was going to yell, I was going to yell even louder.

And if he was going to raise a fist to the crowd, I was going to raise *two* fists to the crowd - horn and all!

Screw trying to prove to others that I belonged, I was going to prove it to *myself*.

There was only one problem.

“Oxygen! Oxygen!

I need more oxygen!

Oh, God – oxygen!

Ox – y – geeeeen...!”

Digga-Digga-DUM! Digga-Digga-DUM! DUM – DUM – *DUM*!

"Up!"

By the end of Entry, my lungs were already threatening a walkout and we hadn't even started playing yet.

But as Cavendish gathered the air around him like some Merlin of Marchology for the most awe-inspiring downbeat I'd ever seen him throw – all while standing atop the same ladder I had schlepped into the stadium the day before as a Reserve – I, too, gathered the air, every spare O2 molecule within 15 yards – and managed to belt – nay, *crank* – my first middle "A" of the New World Order.

There was no going back now.

I was going to play – every – note.

Of course, standing and playing the "Fanfare" was one thing...

...*marching* and playing "The Victors" was another.

In its most rudimentary terms, the sequence went something like this:

1. Lock.
2. Play.
3. Asphyxiate.

Remember when I asked you to put down the book and try out The Lock for yourself? Well, sprint around the block a few times, then try it again--

--*while blowing up an air mattress.*

I guess I could try to describe what it felt like in more conventional terms, but instead I'll tell you what it looked like, progressively, in terms of my face:

Crimson.

Brake Light Crimson.

Satanic Sunburn Brake Light Crimson.

I-Can't-Believe-He's-Not-Dead-Yet Crimson.

Is-It-Humanly-Possible-To-Pass-Into-The-*Infra*red Crimson.

I was now so *deep* into the red, that I was teetering on the edge of meltdown.

There's no way I could keep this up. Just no way. I wasn't going to make it. I wasn't going to be able to play – every – note.

And then it happened.

"Hail! (To the) Victors Valiant! Hail! To the Conquering Heroes...!"

I couldn't believe it! On the chorus of "The Victors"! It happened right next to me, less than 3 feet away, Marko blasting out his 1st trumpet part with such volume that it could actually be heard above 274 other instruments while we swept back upfield from the student endzone!

Can you *believe* it?

I couldn't believe it. You saw it, didn't you? You heard it. You *caught* it...

Didn't you?

Okay, okay, maybe I got wrapped up in the moment and didn't... here, let's go back a minute. The Band had just completed its turn and repositioned itself in the student endzone and were about to step off upfield while playing the one part of the one song that everybody in the entire stadium wanted to hear, our fight song, “The Victors”.

Now, the chorus starts off with “Hail! To the Victors Valiant! Hail! To the Conquering Heroes...!” which everybody in the stands is singing – led by the trumpet section – and *Marko* plays

“Hail! (To the) Victors Valiant! Hail! To the Conquering Heroes...!”

Do you see it now? Do you get it?

I sure did. There was no way I couldn’t. I was marching right next to the guy, and there was no doubt whatsoever:

Marko took a breath!

He missed a couple beats of “The Victors”!

He completely *rested* on the first “To the” before “Victors Valiant”!

I couldn’t believe it.

He didn’t play – two – notes!

I just couldn’t believe it. The man with the leather lungs and thunder thighs, the 1st Chair of the premiere section of the MMB, the Leader of the premiere rank of the premiere marching band in the country...

...and I was up on him by two notes!

The realization brought me a whole new second wind...!

...which lasted about three measures. Then I was back to gulping air on a strict ratio of one agonized breath per note.

Or “blat”.

But there was no way I was going to stop now. I would Lock and Die if necessary, but at least they'd have to chisel into my tombstone

"He played – every – note."

Through the remainder of "The Victors"...

Through the visiting team's fight song, where the fans expected you to miss notes...

Through the trumpet-tensive "Star Spangled Banner" where all around me I could hear the gasps of those who no longer cared if our flag was still there...

"Drop!"

To the merciful interlude for post-anthem applause before we would hear just four more whistles and could get off the field and *receive immediate medical attention.*

I'm not kidding.

I was actually *trying* to hyperventilate to stave off what seemed to be an impending total collapse of my respiratory system.

TWEET! TWEET! TWEET! TWEET!

"Up!"

GASP! GASP!

Lock!

One more "Victors". One more "Victors"...

There it was, I could see it, the finish line – the sideline – just ahead...

One more “Victors”. One more “Victors”...

I was gonna make it. I was gonna make it. I was gonna prove to myself that I belonged here, that I deserved this. I was gonna—

Now, I don’t actually remember passing out. What I do remember are two blurred colors, slowly fading into focus above me:

Yellow and Blue.

“Look...”

“I think he’s coming to...”

“His eyes are opening...”

The colors belonged to plumes. The plumes of Band members bending over me on all sides.

And they brought to mind a question I still hadn’t answered yet.

“Are you all right?”

I managed to sit up along the sideline. Pregame had apparently just concluded and the entire Block now surrounded me, pressing in, sharing my sense of uncertainty and wondering what was going to happen next...

There are moments in your life that balance on a knife’s edge. That can fall either way.

Hero or goat...

No one moved. No one knew what to do. Which to pick. Was I to be brought back into the fold, or left outside? Cheered or booed?

Hero or goat...

This moment couldn't last. The knife edge would fall. Which way would it cut?

Hero or goat...

And sometimes, the nudge that decides it all comes from the highest of powers:

George – R. – Cavendish.

Stepping in.

Beatifically severe in his director's uniform. He stared down at me with furrowing brow and penetrating eyes and then carved into marching lore his mighty pronouncement:

"Now that's giving 150 goddamn percent!"

And like he had just given a baton-free upbeat, the Michigan Marching Band waited exactly one quarter rest before erupting in the day's loudest – and sweetest – music:

"YEAHHHHHHHHHH...!"

I found myself floating to my feet amidst a flurry of white gloves, lifting, patting, molding, sculpting...

Redefining.

Redefining me with their hands.

And when the crowd actually took up the cheer--

"YEAHHHHHHHHHH...!"

--I knew things would never be the same again.

Because after that, I became something of a touchstone for the Michigan Marching Band. Sort of a talisman of good luck.

From that day forward, my place in The Block was secure.

"Way to go, Will."

Dom the Drum Major. Upgrading me to a smile.

To have subjected me to another Challenge would have been unthinkable. I had already undergone The Ultimate...

"Congratulations, Will."

The trumpet Reserve who had been marching in my spot. Now shaking my hand.

...and I had won.

Even Marko couldn't help but acknowledge what had just happened...

"Oof...!"

...after being nudged sharply by a 300-pound lineman leading some of the other football players in applause.

But the topper was still to come.

Taking me by surprise, I suddenly left my feet altogether and began to rise into the air, planted firmly upon the epauletted shoulders of nascent marching immortals who would not soon forget this day.

And as I straightened and rose further still into the crystalline Blue of that early autumn sky, and *saw* the brilliant unfiltered light of the future--

And *heard* the 100,000 hosannas of this new stadial universe--

And *felt* for the first time in my life the very nature of Ur-love--

And... and...

...and you're not really buying any of this, are you?

Come on – the shoulder carry? You really believe that happened?

Oh, uh, by the way, there's a new federal law that just went into effect where everybody who reads this book has to send an extra five bucks directly to me, the writer, at the following address, get a pencil, 3-1-3 North – come on.

People in the stands started to unfurl a "We (heart) Will!" banner.

None of the stuff you're reading now is true.

Photographers came out of nowhere and started flashing snapshots.

So why am I still writing it?

POP! Confetti and streamers.

Because that's the way it should have happened.
Everybody should have a moment like that in their lives.
A storybook moment.

Lights. Cameras. Microphones.

But The Truth is rarely so dramatic.
Are you ready for it?
Here it is:
I never even got Challenged until my <u>second</u> year in marching band.
And I survived.

Cheerleaders. Lots and lots of cheerleaders.

But that wouldn't have been much of a story, would it?

Even though the lessons were just the same.

And what exactly were those lessons?

Finally, with goalposts tumbling, I bowed my head and received a long overdue blue-ribboned medal – and a kiss – from none other than Jeannie Winterspoon.

What was the point of all this?

Scene 4: The Truth

A nice day at school.

I'm back on the Diag, the place on campus where two major diagonal walkways intersect to form an "X", a central crossroads. Only I'm not alone, like the first time I was here. There are people all over the place now, coming and going and everybody moving. And not a single squirrel in sight.

It's the first week of classes.

Freshman Orientation is over.

Back then, when I first started writing all this stuff down, I thought this was going to be just another coming-of-age story.

I do a lot of those.

You know, the transition from high school to college, away from home for really the first time, all condensed down and intensified into a single week – Hell Week – in the Michigan Marching Band. I thought it might make an interesting tale.

A very personalized coming-of-age tale.

In fact, to let you know, here was the final image I was going to use:

So I'm crossing the Diag and I see this kid standing out in front of the same glass door I was standing out in front of just about a week ago and couldn't open. Because it's locked (it's always locked, by the way). And this kid is carrying a campus map.

So I walk over – definitely a Frosh, might as well be wearing a sign – and point him in the right direction.

You see?

Symmetry.

But not Closure.

What do I mean by "Closure"? Well, I'll give you an example. Not only is it the closest we're going to get to a perfect storybook moment...

...it's also True.

But first we need to skip forward a little to springtime, where I was taking an extra "half-term" to get ahead in credits. Specifically, the class was--

"The Second Law states that for all reactions in all systems, open or closed, the entropy – or disorder, 's' – always increases."

--well, boring.

Though technically it was called "Thermodynamics".

Though I guess by that time, at the end of my Freshman year, I was sort of an expert in entropy. Because even though Thermo was taken mostly by seniors who needed a technical elective to graduate, I had managed the highest bluebook scores in class. I bring this up not to brag – well, okay, that, too – but mostly because--

THUMP!

Not unlike the sound I had heard almost nine months before, as I stood for the very first time in The Block of the MMB.

THUMP!

Then, it had been the footstep of my Jurassic Rank Leader.

THUMP!

Now, it was the heel of a palm being pounded into a desktop in frustration.

Though both originated from the same source.

THUMP-THUMP-THUMP!

Marko.

He sat a few rows behind me, supposedly trying to get his mechanical pencil to work. But it was more than that.

Marko was having trouble in Thermodynamics.

He was one of those engineering seniors who had put it off for too long and now needed to pass the class to graduate.

Not my problem, right?

THUMP!

Wrong.

There he was, after class one day, towering directly in front of my desk.

Asking for my help...

...and me, later, actually giving it to him.

Why?

Well, let's just say that 5th year seniors were not unknown in the Michigan Marching Band.

Besides there was even a better reason.

Without going into too much detail, thermodynamic calculations of entropy involved a certain step called--

“Did you lock in the variable?”

“Uhhhhh...”

“Come on, Marko, where’s The Lock? *Where’s* The Lock...?”

Marko got it.

And marched quietly to a passing grade.

I guess every rule has an exception. Because instead of growing and growing without hope and without limit in direct violation of the Second Law of Thermodynamics, the entropy, ‘s’ – the disorder in *this* system...

“Come on, Marko. We do – *every* – calculation.”

...provided “Closure”.

And that’s The Truth.

Well. More or less.

That is, some things were stretched. Like the plumes that went in your hat were more like 12 inches instead of 18. But 18 was a better number for a coming-of-age story. And some things were condensed. Like kickoffs were scheduled for 12:15PM instead of 12:00PM. But “high noon and a quarter” didn’t *ring* true.

A lot of things were exact, though – Chair 74, Rank 82, the 275-member Michigan Marching Band – and everything else that wasn’t...

...was as close as I could get.

And *that's* The Truth.

As for the rest of the story...

Scene 5: The Theme

Time. TWEET! To. TWEET! Wrap. TWEET! Things. TWEET!

"Up!"

(beat) BANG! (beat) BANG! (beat)

"Lock!"

Back to the first week of classes.

But the *second* week of Band.

Rehearsals now take place only from 4:20PM – 6:15PM, though, of course, to be early is to be on time and to be on time is to be late. Every single weekday. For two meager credits.

But I don't mind:

"FIRE UP! IT'S MONDAY!"

"Thor, I am asking - yes or no, please - is it not unreasonable for me to wish to choke a certain rookie Freshman who insists on shouting and sweeping in a manner that requires - at minimum - parity from those on either side of him who may not wish to shout and sweep in such a manner, and to do this thing with my own two bare hands?

"He's not a rookie anymore, Charlie."

"WOO...!"

"Sniff. They grow so very fast..."

When I look back on it now, the most amazing thing to me isn't that I survived, but that I got there at all.

That, in fact, is what this story is *really* all about.

It's called "The Theme", and in contemporary story-telling terms is often defined as – quote – "that thing we usually don't bother too much with" – unquote.

Well, I'm going to bother.

Any ideas as to what it is? The Theme?

Here, I'll give you a hint...

"Dupple commaaaaand!"

Remember this guy? He was slight and prematurely balding, and had some kind of odd, modulating... trans-Anglo accent?

"A-teeen-shut! A-teeen-shut! Uh-One...! Uh-Two...! Uh-Three...!"

That's right. Drum Major Tryouts.

Some of you may have wondered back then why I spent so much time on this since it didn't really seem to have anything to do with the story.

Well, the fact is, it has *everything* to do with the story.

There I am, sitting on the cool grassy sideline with the rest of the Band, trying not to snicker while this guy sweats it up on the asphalt in his own private version of Attention.

There we all are, finally letting go, just laughing at this guy.

And for the longest time, I really thought of him as just some tragic loser.

Standing there in marbleized defiance of dignity, holding his out-sized, non-regulation baton. Just some odd tragic loser...

But I know different now.

I didn't realize it until years later – not until I started writing down this story, in fact – but what this kid did that day is *exactly* what I took away from my marching band experience.

He sweat.

He blinked.

He flushed red.

See, it has to do with doing things you're scared to do. Doing things when the odds are against you. Doing things that everyone else thinks you shouldn't.

And even while I was sitting there snickering, somewhere else, much deeper down, buried under layers of self-consciousness for later retrieval – much *much* later – I began to notice another quality of this rigid, unblinking loser.

Something nobler.

He came. He saw. He failed.

Veni, vidi, ouchie.

It all has to do with The Theme of my story and here it is:

"The greatest tragedy isn't trying and failing,
but never trying at all."

Too obvious?

Too simple?

Too bad.

Because that's what it is. It took me a long, long time to realize it. And I'll bet there are one or two of you out there who could still benefit from the lesson, even if it *is* delivered with pen and sledgehammer.

Now, usually, of course, you're not supposed to just outright *state* The Theme of your story.

It's too blunt.

It's bad form.

It's just not done.

THE THEME

"The greatest tragedy isn't trying
and failing,
but never trying at all."

That's The Theme of "My Marching Band Story".

Lock, lock, lock.

It's how I became a member of one of the best bands in the country.

Lock, lock.

It's how I stayed a member of one of the best bands in the country.

Lock.

And...

Epilogue

...it's how I wrote a book about being a member of one of the best bands in the country.

Okay, a short book.

But still.

TWEEEEEEEEEET!

Final whistle.

The Block slowly dissolves from the field.

Fading now.

Gone.

And with it, Will.

Band was a long time ago...

After graduation, I (the Storyteller "I" now) (with all the parentheticals) (remember?) went to work as an engineer. Aerospace, to be specific, moving even farther away from home to Los Angeles and working with NASA. But I didn't stay an engineer for long. I started writing stories. Scripts, to be specific, both for television and the movies.

But the one story I wanted to most tell I couldn't get told.

Nobody was interested in a week in the life of a kid in marching band. At least, not enough to make a movie, which takes a lot of other people's money.

So I wrote other people's stories.

I've never been back to Michigan Stadium. Or our rehearsal hall. Or the place I remember best, a simple parking lot of tar.

At least, not in person.

Yet I've revisited many times. Over and over again, in fact. Trying to sort things out. Light fading, perimeters growing dim. Until only one thing remained. Persistent, but even that beginning to waver.

A single flag, fluttering at midfield.

And I finally know why:

The telling of my marching band story had become my new Jeannie Winterspoon.

Until now.

And now there's something else standing at midfield.

Five patches sewn up a sleeve, each individually embroidered, two with roses, two without, one that even says "Super Bowl".

Down across the chest a larger patch, a musical lyre bent to form the shape of an "M" and bearing the words, "Michigan Marching Band".

Next to it, the stitching still fresh and vibrant, two more words:

Todd

Trumpet

And finally, somewhere deep in the lining:

"The greatest tragedy isn't trying and failing,
but never trying at all."

And if that's too much to remember, I can sum it all up in just one word.

So when you're stuck, you'll know how to get your feet moving again.

So when you're deciding whether or not to try something you think you'd really like to try, you'll have the key to The Lock.

So when you hear the whistles, you'll know what to do.

I want to tell you.

No, I got to tell you.

No, I *gotta* tell you--

TWEET! TWEET! TWEET! TWEET...!

“March!”

And now the story's told.

BONUS: SCREENPLAY

I (this is the author talking!) didn't start as a novelist, but as a scriptwriter. Similarly, "THE TELLING OF MY MARCHING BAND STORY" didn't start as a book, but as a screenplay.

Which I've decided to include below.

Why?

1. As A Curiosity: For those who have never seen a screenplay before, the following will serve to ease the introduction, since the strangeness of the format will be somewhat offset by the familiarity of the story.

2. As A Primer: For those who have a genuine interest in scriptwriting (i.e., are not actually affiliated with Hollywood), comparing the screenplay to the book - even though the process in this case was reversed - will offer some illumination on the process of adaptation.

3. As A Bonus: Mostly, I just wanted to include something "extra" with my first book. As a way of saying "thanks" for reading it. Something different. Something unique.

Something that showed that, years after the events of this story...

...I'm still marching.

FADE IN:

ON CRYSTAL BLACK SILENCE

as WHITE BLOCK LETTERS BURN INTO THE SCREEN:

Most of what you are about to see is true.

FOLLOWED BY

And where it isn't...

THEN FINALLY

...I'll let you know.

TWEET! TWEET! TWEET! TWEET!

250 VOICES

Hup!

SMASH CUT TO:

A SNARE DRUM

DETONATING a double-time ENTRY CADENCE that drives

THE TITLE SEQUENCE:

Drumsticks blur. Brass and silver flash. Colorful uniforms assemble piece by piece as

LINES begins to form. Curves. Organized patterns in human pointillism. Letters. Words. This being the Title Sequence, you can probably guess what's coming...

...but you'd be only 3/4 right.

HIGH ANGLE - THE MARCHING BAND

standing in "MARCHING BAND STORY" formation. But it's not

until the dot of the "i" skitters upward and unfolds a sign with the word "My" that the title is complete, and the FINAL OPENING CREDIT can roll.

TWEEEEEEEEEET!

The band scatters, quickly forming

"FADE" and "IN:"

My Marching Band Movie can now begin.

TITLE CARD: "ACT ONE: Fresh Man"

CUT TO:

THE FRESHMAN

eighteen and intimidated - and surrounded by

EXT. A LARGE COLLEGE CAMPUS - DAY

where he walks alone:

NARRATOR (V.O.)
My name is Todd.
(beat)
Well, okay, right away, I've gotta tell ya that's not exactly true. There's actually a few "me's" you're gonna have to keep straight here. Three, to be exact.

The Freshman reconnoiters, a folder tucked under his arm.

NARRATOR (V.O.)
First of all, there's Me, The Storyteller. I'm the guy who wrote all this stuff, and my name really is Todd.

The Freshman peeks inside his folder, then turns like a compass needle to follow a new direction.

NARRATOR (V.O.)

Second, there's *Me*, The Narrator. I'm the guy reading all this stuff because I've got a professional voice and Todd doesn't. Don't worry about my name, though.

The Freshman reverses direction.

NARRATOR (V.O.)

And third, there's Me, The Character. I'm the guy on screen right now but you'll have to wait to find out my name because it's not exactly Todd, either, and things are getting complicated enough as it is. So, to summarize...

The Freshman heads toward an imposing building.

NARRATOR (V.O.)

Here's the truth: My name is Todd, but this isn't my voice or my picture. But this *is* my story. Clear?

The Freshman tries to open a clear glass door, but finds it locked. However, its RATTLING may strike a comedically sympathetic chord with the audience at the moment.

NARRATOR (V.O.)

Good. Then here we go...

CLOSE ON - THE FRESHMAN

who turns away from the door looking lost and confused.

NARRATOR (V.O.)

Meet William Todd. Will is lost. Will is confused. Why is Will lost and confused? Because several weeks ago, Will made the biggest mistake of his young life.

(beat)

He graduated from High School.

Hunching over his folder, Will consults a campus map.

NARRATOR (V.O.)
He then compounded his error by deciding to attend the college of his choice.

INSERT - THE MAP

covered with hieroglyphic icons:

NARRATOR (V.O.)
Now this particular college of choice happens to be The University of Michigan because that's where I went to college. But if you'd rather think of it as someplace else, go ahead. They all look pretty much the same at this level anyway.

RESUME ON WILL - on a new bearing, stealing glances at his map as if he might be busted by Campus Navigational Police.

NARRATOR (V.O.)
While actual classes were still weeks away, the wily framers of the Freshman Orientation Program knew they had just two days to strip Will of all self-confidence.

Will approaches another building.

NARRATOR (V.O.)
There were many ways to achieve this goal, but one of the best was to supply Will with a map that would have made Lewis and Clark late for Freshman Chem.

Will reaches another clear glass door, pulls the handle, and... opens it, entering the

INT. BUILDING

where he makes his way down a hall.

NARRATOR (V.O.)
Fortunately, as far as our story is concerned, there was only one really important place that Will had to find...

Double-checking a room number with his folder, Will stops in front of a solid wooden door. Satisfied, he reaches for the knob, pulls, and--

It opens.

Onto a janitorial closet.

NARRATOR (V.O.)
Perhaps a cut would be in order...

CUT TO:

INT. LARGE ROOM (C.R.I.S.P.) - DAY

where in contrast to the desolate confusion of campus, Will now finds himself amidst the DIN of INSTITUTIONALIZED CONFUSION.

NARRATOR (V.O.)
Here we are. Before you see why this place is important, though, I need to come clean about that closet thing. It never really happened. It was just a joke I threw in to cap the sequence. But from now on I'm gonna try and keep that kind of stuff to a minimum. And who knows? By the time we get to the end of the story...
(beat)
...the truth may even be enough. Anyway, welcome to C.R.I.S.P.

Will stands packed in a line that stretches down a stairway into Escher infinity. He awaits a turn at one of the desks that ring the ancient room, each equipped with a computer, counselor, and despairing freshman.

NARRATOR (V.O.)
This is where freshmen were first introduced to the subtle art of class scheduling.

A SOFT CRY OF ANGUISH draws Will's attention to a corner desk, which receives a freshman's forehead with a THUD.

NARRATOR (V.O.)
C.R.I.S.P. supposedly stood for "Computer Registration Involving Student Participation" - though there were other theories...

Will glances at the C.R.I.S.P. worksheet of the freshman in front of him - where the words "Registration" and "Participation" have been crossed out in favor of "Reaming" and "Posterior".

NARRATOR (V.O.)
Philosophy major.

Will returns to his own worksheet.

VOICE
You signing up for MMB?

Will turns, startled, to the GUY IN LINE behind him.

WILL
Oh, uh... I don't know, I just... put it down...

Embarrassed, he hastily crosses it out.

GUY IN LINE
You know, you can sign up now and just drop it if you don't make the audition. That's what I'm gonna do.

WILL
Oh. Well. Hm...

NARRATOR (V.O.)
This'd probably be a good time to point out that it's sort of an unwritten rule in movies that narration be kept to an absolute minimum...

WILL

Mm.

NARRATOR (V.O.)

...that you should let your characters tell the story...

Will turns away with a final, resounding

WILL

Mm.

NARRATOR (V.O.)

Iiiiiiiii don't think so.

Will shuffles forward in line.

NARRATOR (V.O.)

Just think of this like someone reading you a bedtime story. Only the pictures move...

But movement ceases when Will reaches the head of the line, waiting for a calcified old man on a stool to point out the next available station. Time passes. Glaciers approach.

NARRATOR (V.O.)

Perhaps a cut would be in-- ah.

The old man uncrooks a finger and Will follows the point to a desk just vacated by a paler, but CRISPer freshman.

Will sits and hands his worksheet to the battle-hardened COUNSELOR, who begins TYPING it into her computer.

NARRATOR (V.O.)

While Will's waiting here, let me make just one last technical adjustment. Since I have to tell so much of the story, I'm gonna switch from Third Person to First. That means instead of saying "Will did this, Will did that", I'm gonna start saying "I did this, I did that". It's simpler. And kind of truer, too.

(beat)

So here's my first First Person line of narration. Pay attention, it's pretty character revealing...

CLOSE ON - WILL

waiting anxiously for a C.R.I.S.P verdict as the Narrator CLEARS HIS THROAT:

NARRATOR (V.O.)
As usual, I was prepared for the worst. Kids were being locked out of classes left and right...
(Will looks left and right)
...but I had backups, I had permission slips, I had small, unmarked bills. There was only one thing I wasn't prepared for...

BEEP! The computer.

WILL
What.

COUNSELOR
You got all your classes.

WILL
Really?

The Counselor returns to TYPING as Will sinks back into his chair, smiling.

NARRATOR (V.O.)
An incredible stroke of luck. <u>All</u> the classes I wanted...

But in sitting back, Will spots a poster on the wall beside him. It depicts a blue uniformed leg at perfect right angle and tempts: "Michigan Marching Band!"

Will's smile fades.

NARRATOR (V.O.)
It was a sign. I mean, not just a sign-sign, but...

COUNSELOR
(re: worksheet)
Wait a minute, is this something down here - "MMB"...? Did you want to add this?

Will rises slowly - majestically - from his seat.

NARRATOR (V.O.)
And so, hearing my call to destiny, I did what I've always done when confronted with stark opportunity...

WILL
(shaking head)
No.

And as the Counselor RIPS Will's schedule from a printer and hands it over

CUT TO:

EXT. REVEILLE MUSIC HALL - (ANOTHER) DAY

where Will stands with instrument case reading a banner: "Michigan Marching Band - Auditions Today".

NARRATOR (V.O.)
I guess I've got some explaining to do.

While others stream past, Will slowly climbs the steps and enters the

INT. LOBBY

where he receives directions at a check-in table.

NARRATOR (V.O.)

It's not that I changed my mind about auditioning, really, it's just that... in the long, slow, summer weeks that followed orientation, I kept wondering about it, and thinking about it, and... and...

Will passes through a set of double doors into

THE CAVERNOUS MAIN REHEARSAL HALL

NARRATOR (V.O.)

...and fearing it.

Eyes wide, he takes in the hanger-sized temple, built on the epauletted shoulders of marching immortals. And alumni funds.

NARRATOR (V.O.)

But it wasn't until I was standing in the great rehearsal hall, balanced on the threshold of tradition...

Will stumbles forward with a GRUNT, bumped aside by the entrance of a muscle mass in the shape of an UPPERCLASSMAN.

NARRATOR (V.O.)

...that I knew those fears had been well-founded.

WILL

Sorry...

The Upperclassman just glares, joining a click of his fellows. Though they all share the same size instrument case, Will is teenage lightyears removed from this group. He gives them a wide berth, trying to stay outside the perimeter of their eyes.

NARRATOR (V.O.)

It was like being the new grunt in 'Nam. Nobody wanted to get too close, too soon...

Will retreats to the back of the room and sits on his case.

NARRATOR (V.O.)

...just in case you didn't make it...

And for the first time, he takes a good look at the seats on the floor - arranged in a giant circle, facing outward.

NARRATOR (V.O.)

...in the biggest game of musical chairs ever played.

DISSOLVE TO:

SAME SCENE - LATER

now filled with cases and their owners. The veterans are easy to spot, congregated in pockets of bravado, while the newcomers, including Will, pretty much suffer alone.

None, however, has taken a seat in the forbidden circle. Most, in fact, try to avoid even looking at it. Until:

TWEET!

VOICE

All right, listen up!

All eyes turn to the whistle - which wears a Norman Rockwell painting under its neck cord entitled:

"DRUM MAJOR"

My name's Guy and right now I want you all to take a seat in the approximate chair position you think you're gonna end up in. Firsts start over here, thirds end over here. Let's go, this is it.

It's as if a starter's pistol has been fired. Will once again finds people streaming past him.

NARRATOR (V.O.)

The sudden reality took me a bit by surprise, but this was actually one of the easier decisions...

Will heads straight for the bottom third of the circle, sits, reconsiders, then moves a little further down toward the end. He's quickly bookended by two other players, and involuntarily stiffens when, around the room, the CLICKING of case locks go off like a smattering of gunfire.

NARRATOR (V.O.)
I figured there must be at least 80 guys here, and even if each audition only took a couple minutes...

DRUM MAJOR
Ten minutes to warm up!

Will nervously raises his own battered case to his lap.

NARRATOR (V.O.)
Still, it was all happening so fast an' I was starting to feel actually sick an' you've gotta be asking yourself right about now why? Why was I doing this...?

Will CLICKS open his case locks. One needs a manual assist.

NARRATOR (V.O.)
Well, to have a chance at understanding that, you've gotta first understand this...

Will lifts the case lid, and for the first time REVEALS

THE TRUMPET

cradled in worn red velvet, etched by skin oil and time - a piece of brass whose legacy has been purchased at the expense of its luster.

NARRATOR (V.O.)
...and this is gonna take some explaining.

And as Will's hands invoke the familiar metal

MATCH DISSOLVE TO:

THE SAME TRUMPET

only now the hands are much smaller and the metal gleams, brand new. It rises from its case to greet

YOUNG WILL

who works the valves as if performing magic.

NARRATOR (V.O.)
Like most kids, I started playing an instrument in about the 4th grade.

FREEZE FRAME

NARRATOR (V.O.)
By the way, I know this kid doesn't look anything like me, but he won't be around for long, so just pretend, okay?

RESUME

on Young Will, looking around:

NARRATOR (V.O.)
This meant applying the full force of 9-year-old logic to choose the optimal instrument. Percussion...

ON THE PERCUSSION SECTION

of an Elementary School beginner's band - where bass and snare are less played than assaulted.

NARRATOR (V.O.)
(petulant)
...dumb. Woodwinds...

ON THE WOODWIND SECTION

where a variety of reeds all play the same note: SQUEAK!

NARRATOR (V.O.)
...stupid. Brass...

ON THE BRASS SECTION

bright, shiny - and loud.

NARRATOR (V.O.)
...cool. But this still left some choices. Tuba...

ON A TUBA PLAYER

already developing the requisite obesity, but still young enough to be crushed by his instrument if careless.

NARRATOR (V.O.)
...which I could never think of without the words "tragic" and "accident". Trombone...

ON A TROMBONE

GLISSANDOING through the no-man's-land between notes.

NARRATOR (V.O.)
Now these guys *thought* they were cool, but how cool could you be with an overgrown version of the whistle you used to get in Cracker Jacks? No, there was only one *truly* cool instrument in band...

BACK ON YOUNG WILL

reflected in the bell of his

NARRATOR (V.O.)
Trumpet. Why would anyone play anything else? All the notes in the world you could want right at your fingertips in just three little valves.
(beat)
Of course, there was one catch...

Young Will removes a mouthpiece from the case and gently twists it into his horn.

NARRATOR (V.O.)
See, in a real trumpet, to produce any kind of sound, you can't just blow...

Young Will carefully positions his lips and takes a breath.

NARRATOR (V.O.)
...you have to buzz.

Which is about the best way to describe the - to be generous - SOUNDS coming from Young Will's horn. Kind of like a rusty turboprop struggling to life on bad gas.

NARRATOR (V.O.)
The French call this "embouchure", meaning "the position and use of the lips to produce a musical tone" - and besides being another reason to hate the French, "embouchure" was to become my personal demon in the trumpet years ahead. For now, though...

Young Will manages to force an actual note from his instrument. He beams.

NARRATOR (V.O.)
...I was happy. Everything was promise, hope, and potential.

On the music stand in front of him, Young Will opens "Easy Steps To The Band" and finds a page filled with wide staffs and open, friendly notes.

NARRATOR (V.O.)
Music was simple...

MATCH CUT TO:

ANOTHER STAND

as a small piece of music SLAPS into place, almost black with notes by comparison.

NARRATOR (V.O.)
...but, of course, that couldn't last.

INT. REVEILLE MUSIC HALL

where the Drum Major continues to SLAP copies of the audition piece onto stands until he reaches the end of the circle, and hence the beginning:

DRUM MAJOR
Again, you'll play Intro to Letter B, then everyone'll vote to see whether you move up or stay the same. Okay, this is Chair #1...

Though the outward-facing circle is meant to promote anonymity, Will is close enough to the end to see who occupies Chair #1: The same Upperclassman who welcomed him with a bump and a glare. He blows a few preparatory NOTES.

NARRATOR (V.O.)
Well, at least I'd get to hear it about 70 times before I had to--

The thought is interrupted by the start of the AUDITION PIECE. Perhaps it's the speed of the sixteenth note runs, or the sheer power of the Upperclassman's volume, but one result is clear as the music quickly concludes:

Will's eyes have been opened. Wide:

NARRATOR (V.O.)
Check, please?

DRUM MAJOR
Okay, next.

Chair #2 launches into the SAME PIECE, technically perfect, but not nearly as loud. Will, however, continues to squirm.

NARRATOR (V.O.)
What was I doing here? I hated auditions. Always had. Always...

DISSOLVE TO:

INT. JUNIOR HIGH SCHOOL BAND ROOM

where a PREADOLESCENT WILL (Pre-Will) performs with his peers in an all-white, Junior High RENDITION of "Shaft".

NARRATOR (V.O.)
By the time Junior High rolled around, I had acquired a certain level of proficiency.

FREEZE FRAME

NARRATOR (V.O.)
By the way, I realize this kid doesn't look much like me, either, but we needed someone with braces and this was cheaper than trying to fake orthodontics.

RESUME

as Pre-Will PLAYS a run of high notes, then rests, massaging his upper lip and indeed revealing a mouth full of metal.

NARRATOR (V.O.)
This despite a lip that was on the verge of ground chuck. The orthodontist wanted me to quit, or change instruments, but I had made 2nd chair trumpet in 9th grade band, and I was content.
(beat)
Of course, that couldn't last.

A door to a practice stall opens in the back of the room, drawing the eye of Pre-Will. He watches a JUNIOR HIGH TRUMPET return to the empty 1st chair next to him as the JUNIOR HIGH DIRECTOR cuts off the band:

JUNIOR HIGH DIRECTOR
Good. Better. Clarinets...

He turns to address the woodwinds, leaving an opportunity for Trumpet Chairs #1 and #2 to converse in low tones:

PRE-WILL
How'd it go?

JUNIOR HIGH TRUMPET
Okay, I guess. You're next.

PRE-WILL
I know...

Pre-Will solemnly gathers some music and heads back to the practice stall.

NARRATOR (V.O.)
The High School Band Director was here to audition us for next Fall.

JUNIOR HIGH DIRECTOR
Okay, let's move on to our next Theme...

NARRATOR (V.O.)
It was time to face the demon "embouchure" once again.

Now at the stall door, Pre-Will takes a deep breath. And just as he twists the knob

THE BAND STRIKES UP THE THEME FROM "THE EXORCIST"

REVEALING a shadowy figure in dark overcoat and fedora standing in the doorway!

NARRATOR (V.O.)
Sorry. I couldn't resist.

THE DOOR REOPENS, this time revealing a doughy, middle-aged man with a friendly smile:

HIGH SCHOOL DIRECTOR
Will?
(receives a nod)
Come on in. Have a seat.

INT. PRACTICE STALL

where a jittery Pre-Will sits in one of two chairs facing a lone music stand.

HIGH SCHOOL DIRECTOR
Don't worry, I'll try to make this as painless as possible. Why don't we start with a warm-up...?

NARRATOR (V.O.)
I know what you're thinking - nice guy, right?

HIGH SCHOOL DIRECTOR
C scale - two octaves.

NARRATOR (V.O.)
Straight for the jugular.

Pre-Will raises his horn and BEGINS the lower "C" scale.

NARRATOR (V.O.)
What you have to understand is, high "C" is the theoretical limit on a B-flat trumpet - made even more theoretical by the fact that I had never hit one before.

Pre-Will passes middle "C" and ASCENDS timorously into the uncharted upper register.

NARRATOR (V.O.)

Never. Not in six years. And no amount of adrenaline, no amount of arm pressure, no amount of nerve damage to my lip...

Indeed, the mouthpiece seems destined for the back of Pre-Will's head, right up to the moment when...

...he nails the theoretical limit:

NARRATOR (V.O.)

...could explain the Miracle of that moment.

Pre-Will lowers his horn in awe. The High School Director makes a casual note in his folder.

HIGH SCHOOL DIRECTOR

Okay, let's hear some of your prepared piece.

Pre-Will spreads his music out on the stand, dabbing his upper lip with his sleeve.

NARRATOR (V.O.)

It was the only high "C" I ever hit. Ever. And that's the truth. It set me up in the top band in High School. It was not only the highest note I ever played, but the highest point of my entire trumpet career.

Pre-Will looks at his sleeve, now spotted with red.

NARRATOR (V.O.)

And all it had cost was a little blood...

CUT TO:

INT. REVEILLE MUSIC HALL

where Will unconsciously dabs his upper lip with his wrist.

NARRATOR (V.O.)

...which was nothing compared to *this* torture.

A player at mid-circle COMPLETES the audition piece.

DRUM MAJOR

Show of hands, should he move up?

(judging count)

Next.

The next player STARTS the audition piece anew.

NARRATOR (V.O.)

It was like listening to a train approaching. In G major. And being tied to the tracks.

Will fingers along with the music for the umpteenth time.

NARRATOR (V.O.)

Now maybe you're wondering how it could be so bad? After all, I had years of experience - even with auditions. So why the agony?

Will doubles forward but keeps fingering. While there, he spots someone's open instrument case on the floor.

NARRATOR (V.O.)

Well, I guess there's one thing I haven't told you yet...

And as the SHOT TIGHTENS ON HIS NEIGHBOR'S CASE - and the ribboned medals that hang within

BEGIN ANOTHER DISSOLVE, BUT

FREEZE FRAME IN CROSS-FADE:

NARRATOR (V.O.)

By the way, I promise this'll be the last flashback. But at least you'll recognize me in this one.

RESUME DISSOLVE TO:

INT. HIGH SCHOOL BAND ROOM

where Will (just plain Will) and the rest of the band PERFORM that staple of High School repertoire, "2nd Suite in Military F" by Gustav Holst.

NARRATOR (V.O.)
After nine full years of playing in public school, it had come to this: 2nd chair, 1st trumpet, Symphony Band. And I deserved it. I had good tone, strong technique, and an ear for music. It was the best I could have possibly done...
(beat)
...given my shortcomings...

Will belts out an ascending run - but stops short of the highest note.

NARRATOR (V.O.)
There - see? - laid off on the high "A". And here...
(as Will rests)
...after four pretty tough measures, I had to rest for one. Perfect examples of the two areas I had the most trouble: Range and Endurance. Which - I'm sure this is just a coincidence, I'm not blaming god or anything - anymore...

Will glances at the 1st chair trumpet, covering the notes he begs off on.

NARRATOR (V.O.)
...happen to be the two most prized attributes of a trumpet player. And I can show you exactly why I didn't possess them. It's the thing I haven't told you yet. Here it comes:

FREEZE FRAME - CLOSE ON WILL'S MOUTH

as he rests for another measure.

NARRATOR (V.O.)
I have no upper lip.

TELESTRATOR LINES appear on the FRAME.

NARRATOR (V.O.)
The most vital part of a trumpet player's anatomy and - here, I'll circle the area where the alleged lip *should* appear - see? - nothing. We go from nose, across the barren mustache plateau - BOOM - straight to bottom lip.

TELESTRATOR LIPS are now drawn on top of everything else.

NARRATOR (V.O.)
But it's the *upper* lip that does the important buzz work in a mouthpiece. No upper lip? No range, no endurance.

The TELESTRATOR mess disappears, replaced by a question mark.

NARRATOR (V.O.)
Freak of nature? Maybe. But as far as the trumpet was concerned, the Bottom Line was this:

RESUME ON WILL - taking a breath:

NARRATOR (V.O.)
I couldn't - play - every - note.

Will joins back in, still clipping and resting.

NARRATOR (V.O.)
Now, that's not so bad when you're playing in a group. You're covered...

A BELL RINGS and the High School Director cuts everyone off, dismissing them with a smile and a

HIGH SCHOOL DIRECTOR
Fi-ne'.

NARRATOR (V.O.)
But there's one place it doesn't work...

The 1st chair HIGH SCHOOL TRUMPET opens his case...

...and reveals several of the ribboned medals that precipitated this FLASHBACK.

HIGH SCHOOL TRUMPET
You ready for Solo?

Will sours as he opens his own case, medal-free.

WILL
No.

NARRATOR (V.O.)
He was referring to the annual state-wide "Solo and Ensemble Festival" which an unwanted private instructor had insisted I volunteer for in my senior year.

HIGH SCHOOL TRUMPET
You'll be fine.

Will continues to stow his instrument.

NARRATOR (V.O.)
More like "fi-ne"'. I couldn't play every note...

Will looks again at the medals in the 1st chair's case.

NARRATOR (V.O.)
If your performance was judged "excellent" you received a blue ribbon. The red was for "fair". I was the only one in my entire high school that year...

The 1st chair trumpet CLOSES his case.

NARRATOR (V.O.)
...who received no ribbon.

And as Will stares at his own medal-free case

MATCH CUT TO:

THAT SAME CASE

as a hand, shaking visibly, reaches in for some valve oil.

NARRATOR (V.O.)
And I was a lot less nervous then than I was now.

INT. REVEILLE MUSIC HALL

where Will tries to work the eye dropper needed to oil his valves, while the trumpet *directly before him* PLAYS the audition piece.

But Will realizes this is much too delicate work for the state he's in now, and abandons the effort.

NARRATOR (V.O.)
I was a nervous wreck. Worse, I was a nervous wreck with no upper lip.

The player before him CONCLUDES. Will looks like a hunted animal.

NARRATOR (V.O.)
Which brings us back to the question originally posed...

DRUM MAJOR
Should he move up?

NARRATOR (V.O.)
Or put another way...

DRUM MAJOR
(after count)
Next.

NARRATOR (V.O.)

(panicking)

...what was I doing here!? Why? Why was I doing this...?

Will raises the suddenly immense weight of his trumpet.

NARRATOR (V.O.)

And I have an honest answer.

And as Will takes a deep breath

FREEZE FRAME

NARRATOR (V.O.)

I don't know.

RESUME

as Will stumbles into the INTRO of the audition piece - pinched, rushed, erratic - and sounding quite...

FREEZE FRAME

NARRATOR (V.O.)

...Uncertain. But sometimes the truth is simply that: You just don't know. I certainly couldn't have given you one good reason at the time. But even with the advantage of perspective, I'm still not sure.

(beat)

All I can do is offer several possibilities...

RESUME

as Will continues with the 1st PHRASE, two 16th-note runs he should be able to handle, but are turning out to be...

NARRATOR (V.O.)

...Harder than I thought. I mean, maybe I wasn't fully aware of what I was getting into. Maybe I kept a realistic consideration of it walled off in the back of my mind, because I knew if I thought about it too much, I might not go through with it.

RESUME

as Will continues with the 2nd PHRASE - more runs, more problems - or...

FREEZE FRAME

NARRATOR (V.O.)

...More of the same. Meaning, maybe it simply had to do with the fact that I was uprooting my life to start college anyways, and what was one more gut-wrenching, psyche-threatening trauma to add to the list?

RESUME

as Will continues by essentially repeating the 1st PHRASE, which makes things a little...

FREEZE FRAME

NARRATOR (V.O.)

...Easier. In other words, maybe it was just the lesser of two evils. Maybe I would've always wondered if I could've made it, and somehow I knew that would be worse than actually finding out.

RESUME

as Will continues with the 4th and FINAL PHRASE, a long, ascending run that is interrupted by a

FREEZE FRAME just before the last and highest note.

NARRATOR (V.O.)

Take your pick. All I knew at the moment was...

RESUME

as Will TRIES TO HIT THE HIGH NOTE - repeatedly - but keeps sliding off it like the braying of a metallic donkey.

NARRATOR (V.O.)
...I had fallen short.

Will gives up, slowly lowering his horn to half mast.

NARRATOR (V.O.)
At that point, the "why" didn't really matter anymore. What did matter was...

DRUM MAJOR
Should he move up?
(a quick count)
Next.

NARRATOR (V.O.)
I didn't move up.

The next player BEGINS - and sounds just as bad if not worse than Will, who brightens a bit.

NARRATOR (V.O.)
Then again...

SAME SCENE - LATER

as the last chair completes his audition to an indifferent and weary show of hands.

NARRATOR (V.O.)
...I didn't move down, either. After three solid hours of the same 20 seconds of music, most of this group wouldn't have lifted a hand to vote for mandatory sex laws. And so by sheer, tenacious apathy...

DRUM MAJOR
That does it.

NARRATOR (V.O.)

...I ended up in pretty much the same chair I had chosen at the beginning. There was a lesson in there somewhere, but I missed it because of the number 74...

The Drum Major walks up from the bottom of the circle and stops one chair below Will.

DRUM MAJOR

One through 75...

NARRATOR (V.O.)

My Chair Number was 74.

DRUM MAJOR

...congratulations and welcome to the Michigan Marching Band!

Immediately, chairs are evacuated, handshakes exchanged, and pent-up smiles released. Even Will gets to share in some of the sudden CAMARADERIE.

NARRATOR (V.O.)

This is the truth. I had made the band by <u>one</u> chair.

(beat)

The hard part was over.

Will looks at a corner where the Drum Major has gathered those players who didn't make the cut, several of whom...

...look back at Will.

NARRATOR (V.O.)

Or so I thought...

And as a shadow follows Will back to the light of congratulations

DISSOLVE TO:

TITLE CARD: "ACT TWO: Hell Week"

CUT TO:

FLAMES

engulfing the feet of a marcher - as depicted in

A SIGN

that advises "Fire Up! It's..." followed by a slot filled with the word "Monday". The sign hangs inside

INT. REVEILLE MUSIC HALL - (SAME) DAY

where chairs have been returned to standard concert formation and are now filled with eager MUSICIANS.

NARRATOR (V.O.)
There were a lot of catch phrases in marching band. From the topical...

Near the end of the trumpets, Will turns from "Monday" to

ANOTHER SIGN

with the words: "Perfection is made up of trifles. But perfection is no trifle."

NARRATOR (V.O.)
...to the philosophical. It took 15 years before I found out this was a quote from Michelangelo, and not our Drum Major, "Guy".

Will spots the whistle-bound majordomo near the podium, casting nervous glances toward the door.

NARRATOR (V.O.)

But the most important phrase was the favorite of the man who held the baton. The leader of the band. Our director:

CLOSE ON - A HUGE FLAG

which entirely FILLS THE SCREEN - blue, with a yellow "M":

NARRATOR (V.O.)

George - R. - Cavendish.

DRUM MAJOR (O.S.)

Everybody up...!

O.S. chairs SCRAPE, then ALL SOUND CEASES.

AN OLD MAN CLIMBS INTO THE FLAG SHOT, and stands nearly at attention.

And while a TRUMPET BLOWS "Assembly"

A SERIES OF CLOSE-UPS FOLLOWS:

- The Old Man's eyes, piercing;

- The marching band insignia on his chest;

- The ivory baton tucked under his arm like a riding crop.

"Assembly" CONCLUDES.

CAVENDISH

Be seated.

O.S. chairs again SCRAPE, followed by COMPLETE SILENCE.

CAVENDISH

Now... I want you to remember... that no one ever won a spot in this band... by giving less than 150 percent.

They <u>won</u> it... by letting the <u>other</u> poor dumb bastard give less than 150 percent.

NARRATOR (V.O.)

Well, okay, maybe he didn't say "bastard". But you get the idea.

Cavendish steps forward to his music stand.

NARRATOR (V.O.)

And to both the long-acquainted and the newly-converted inside that hall...

ON WILL, slack-jawed.

NARRATOR (V.O.)

...Cavendish was the burning bush of marching band. When he spoke, you took off your shoes and listened.

CAVENDISH

B-flat concert.

His baton giveth, then taketh, life from a TUNING NOTE.

NARRATOR (V.O.)

That's why when he said...

CAVENDISH

Trumpets. One at a time.

NARRATOR (V.O.)

...we merely accepted the fact that we would spend that entire first rehearsal each playing just one note.

The trumpets go down the line, TUNING.

NARRATOR (V.O.)

Cavendish'll become particularly important at the climax of the story. But for now, it was enough to know we had a shepherd who would keep us from getting lost...

CUT TO:

EXT. ELBERT PRACTICE FIELD - (LATER THAT) DAY

where Will and several others wander around, lost.

NARRATOR (V.O.)

Baaaaa, baaaaa...

Will peers at a freshly-copied set of charts.

NARRATOR (V.O.)

Okay, don't panic, let's do this again. Here's "Todd"... Chair Number 74... which translates to Rank Number 82... see Chart "B"...

CLOSE ON - CHART "B"

a legal-sized piece of paper with numbered dots on a grid.

NARRATOR (V.O.)

...which puts me about the middle of the most important formation in all of marching band...

THE CHART LOWERS, REVEALING

NARRATOR (V.O.)

...The Block.

an impressive rectangular assemblage of human rows and columns, laid out by yardline.

NARRATOR (V.O.)

This was where you drilled. This was where you paraded. This... was home.

Will walks along the outskirts of The Block, counting rows.

NARRATOR (V.O.)

And like all homes, the quality of life depended on the neighborhood. My new address was "Rank 8".

Will passes next to a row - or rank - of upperclassmen, who casually stand everywhere but the yardline.

NARRATOR (V.O.)

Nope, wait a minute, I recognized these guys, these were all first trumpets, I must've miscounted...

Reexamining his chart, Will continues past them, but is stopped at the next row by a round-up cry of

RANK 9 LEADER

Rank 9...!

which indicates that Will may not have miscounted after all. Slowly, he looks back at the previous rank.

NARRATOR (V.O.)

No, no, no. This had to be a mistake. A misprint.

(as Will goes off)

I needed to find the guy in cha--

DRUM MAJOR

What's your Block Number?

WILL

Uh, well, according to <u>this</u>, um... 82, but...

The Drum Major takes three quick steps into Rank 8.

DRUM MAJOR

Right here.

Will has no choice but to take his place, alone in a crowd after the DM leaves to pick up other stragglers.

NARRATOR (V.O.)
Now, some people would've been thrilled to be planted in the band's premiere rank. But I was odd man out. Way out. If this was Trumpet Valhalla...

Will looks down the line - and finds an entire rank of dubious upperclassmen leaning forward in a fan of scrutiny.

NARRATOR (V.O.)
...I was Loki, God of the Lipless.

Will unconsciously rubs his upper lip.

NARRATOR (V.O.)
Where was "Thor" when you needed him?

VOICE
Hi, I'm Thor.

Will turns to see

THOR KENDALL

smiling down at him beneficently. Tall. Long blond hair. No hammer, but generally god-like. Everything Will is not.

THOR
You 82?

WILL
Um... well, according to this...

THOR
I'm 81. Welcome to Rank 8.

For a moment, Will can only stare at the outstretched hand.

NARRATOR (V.O.)
Okay, I'll admit the guy's name wasn't really Thor. And... actually... he didn't look much like this, either. But that's the way I like to remember him...

Realizing this isn't a trick, Will shuffles his charts around to grab the hand before him.

NARRATOR (V.O.)
...because that hand was like a life preserver to me. Keeping me afloat on a sea of uncertainty.

THOR
What's your name?

WILL
(too eager)
Will - what's yours?
(realizing)
Oh, you... "Thor", right...

He's saved further embarrassment by a startling TWEET!

DRUM MAJOR (O.S.)
Let's go - everybody find your rank!

THOR
Just hang loose - things won't start getting ugly until the second whistle.

NARRATOR (V.O.)
Thor helped me to see what did - and more importantly, what didn't - have to be taken seriously.

They are interrupted by

CHARLIE GUPTA

a Hindu youth who draws a line just over Will's head while trying, unsuccessfully, to sound stern:

CHARLIE
Oh, I am sorry - but you must be this tall to ride this attraction.

NARRATOR (V.O.)

Charlie, on the other hand, didn't take *anything* seriously.

THOR

Chuckles, this is who'll be keeping us apart this year - Will.

CHARLIE

Homewrecker!

But he says it with such a goofy smile that Will can't help but mirror him.

NARRATOR (V.O.)

Charlie helped keep alive the hope that in some future I could not yet fathom, big-time college marching band might actually be...

TWEET! Thor and Charlie SNAP to attention on either side of Will, who nervously follows suit.

NARRATOR (V.O.)

...non-bladder-threatening. But at least wedged between the #2 and #3 trumpets in band...

DRUM MAJOR (O.S.)

Anyone who has <u>not</u> found their rank - speak now!

NARRATOR (V.O.)

...I had found my place in The Block.

Will almost grins.

NARRATOR (V.O.)

All I had to do was follow my bookends to stay out of trouble.

DRUM MAJOR (O.S.)

Rank leaders! Inspection!

NARRATOR (V.O.)

They had been doing this for three years. They were the best the band had to offer.

A DULL THUMP! like a sandbag hitting the field wipes the grin from Will's face.

NARRATOR (V.O.)

But I was wrong...

Another, closer THUMP!

NARRATOR (V.O.)

As good as they were...

Another THUMP! causes Will's horn to vibrate. It's like a scene from "Jurassic Park".

NARRATOR (V.O.)

...there was someone better.

A final THUMP! draws Will's eyes down to the field where

TWO SIZE 16 SHOES

settle toe-to-toe with Will's size 8's. THE SHOT SLOWLY RISES past gargantuan, hairy legs:

NARRATOR (V.O.)

He was a tireless marcher. It was as if the Japanese had designed one of those transformer-bots with fuel tanks that morphed into thighs.

THE SHOT CONTINUES RISING to the chest:

NARRATOR (V.O.)

He was a powerful player. His lungs could blow more wind than Congress. And to top it all off...

THE SHOT FINALLY REVEALS a square, blunt, glowering face:

NARRATOR (V.O.)
...he hated my living guts.

The face, however, is familiar. It belongs to the same Upperclassman who bumped into Will before auditions.

REVERSE ON WILL, who swallows hard.

NARRATOR (V.O.)
He was Rank Leader. He was 1st Chair Trumpet. He was, simply...

RESUME EVEN TIGHTER on the face of the JV Schwarzenegger:

THOR (O.S.)
Marko.

MARKO
(without turning)
What.

THOR (O.S.)
You're supposed to inspect me first.

MARKO
(now turns)
You're at attention, Thor.

Thor returns to attention. If it were ever in doubt, it's now clear where authority lies. Will swallows again.

NARRATOR (V.O.)
I was never to know exactly why Marko hated my living guts. It was just one of those whims of nature you couldn't explain, like tornados and trailer parks.

Marko continues to glare at the small trailer before him.

NARRATOR (V.O.)
I ran down several lines of thought, though. Number One...

LINE OF THOUGHT #1 is represented by a QUICK DOLLY down the length of Rank 8, past several backs-of-heads until a space appears, and the SHOT MUST ABRUPTLY FRAME DOWN to find Will.

NARRATOR (V.O.)
...I was a freshman. Everyone else in Rank 8 was an upperclassman. Number Two...

LINE OF THOUGHT #2 follows another QUICK DOLLY of the rank, this time past flashy silver trumpets before braking in front of Will's own brass memorial.

NARRATOR (V.O.)
...I was a third trumpet. Everyone else in Rank 8 was a first. And lastly, in a rank where everyone else was keeping cool...

A LAST QUICK DOLLY past shorts and bare legs ends in pants:

NARRATOR (V.O.)
...I wasn't.

It's a distinction that hasn't been lost on

MARKO
(re: charts)
"(t)odd"...

Hearing his last name pronounced with a purposeful emphasis on the "odd", Will opts for silence and a third swallow.

MARKO
We don't wear "pants" in the Michigan Marching Band, "(t)odd". Especially...

He looks down.

NARRATOR (V.O.)
Go ahead, say it, <u>say</u> it... Polyester!

MARKO

(darkly)

...during "Hell Week".

One more lingering glare and Marko is gone, moving on to the next in line. Will stares straight ahead.

NARRATOR (V.O.)

It was the first time I'd heard the phrase, but it wouldn't be the last. It's very mention could strike terror into people's hearts...

CHARLIE

Marko, Marko - how does your garden grow?

MARKO

Shut up, Charlie.

CHARLIE

Okay.

NARRATOR (V.O.)

Most people, anyway. And with good reason.

Will allows his eyes to examine The Block in front of him.

NARRATOR (V.O.)

"Hell Week" was the time allotted to transform a block of raw, summer-vacation-bloated recruits into a precision marching machine. And it started with...

CUT TO:

SAME SCENE - LATER

DRUM MAJOR

Everybody up!

MMB

One!

The Block rockets from crouch to attention.

NARRATOR (V.O.)
...learning how to stand up.

DRUM MAJOR
Everybody down...

Will crouches down again, noting how serious everyone is.

NARRATOR (V.O.)
Now, I had been in marching band in High School. It was fun. It was loose. It was...

DRUM MAJOR
Everybody up!

MMB
One!

NARRATOR (V.O.)
...assumed we already knew how to stand up.

DRUM MAJOR
Everybody down...

Will returns to his crouch, cramping a bit.

NARRATOR (V.O.)
But this was the Michigan Marching Band - MMB - where nothing was taken for granted except 150% effort and...

DRUM MAJOR
Everybody up!

MMB
One!

NARRATOR (V.O.)

...no grading on a curve.

To Will's horror, the Drum Major makes a beeline for him...

DRUM MAJOR

You're late! You're late!

...then passes by to chew someone else out.

DRUM MAJOR

Where's the effort? Where's the effort? Everybody down...

Down they go. Will breathes a sigh of relief.

NARRATOR (V.O.)

But standing up for over an hour was cake compared to what came next. It's what set MMB apart from every other marching band in the country...

DRUM MAJOR

Everybody up!

And as The Block springs skyward

MATCH CUT TO:

SAME SCENE - LATER

MMB

One!

as the band stands with left legs frozen at right angles:

NARRATOR (V.O.)

It was called "The Lock".

CLOSE ON - THOR

statufied in textbook Lock:

NARRATOR (V.O.)

Thigh parallel to the ground. Calf perpendicular. Toe pointed. The Lock was to the Michigan Marching Band what bedrock is to...

WIDEN TO INCLUDE - WILL

barely keeping his balance:

NARRATOR (V.O.)

...Los Angeles?

DRUM MAJOR

Attention by the numbers - readyyy, two!

MMB

Two!

The Lock shifts suddenly to the right leg. Will teeters.

NARRATOR (V.O.)

Fortunately, there was one part of this drill at which I excelled...

DRUM MAJOR

Attention by the numbers - readyyy, three!

MMB

Three!

The right leg drives down, leaving everyone at attention and balanced on two feet.

NARRATOR (V.O.)

"Three." Unfortunately, there was another drill that had no "three"...

Four - TWEET! - very - TWEET! - slow - TWEET! - whistles - TWEET! - trigger an

MMB

(horns snapping)

Up!

followed by a single SNARE with preparatory beats and a HUSHED CHANT of "Sweep, sweep, sweep, sweep...!" that climaxes in a cry of

MMB

Lock!

as left legs power up and the entire Block takes off in a

SWEEP DRILL

down the field, each step a sudden right angle held locked until the next will-spaced BANG OF THE SNARE.

Not unlike the galley scene from "Ben Hur".

NARRATOR (V.O.)

Sweeps were a conditioning drill. They were meant to build up muscle and wind while tearing down mental barriers like the will to protest.

The SNARE pushes the tempo, and Will begins to struggle.

NARRATOR (V.O.)

Each step had to be distinct. No bicycling. Change like a piston. That was "The Lock".

(beat)

I suggest you all give it a try after the movie. Only then can you truly understand how "The Lock"...

Will begins to PANT.

NARRATOR (V.O.)

...put the "Hell" in "Hell Week".

(beat)

Although this particular week, there was an even better reason...

And as the SNARE drives on

CUT TO:

THE BELL OF WILL'S TRUMPET

as first one, then several drops SPLASH off its surface. It's owner is down on one knee providing the sweat while the horn provides much-needed head support.

Above, a Lawrence-of-Arabia sun bakes this

SAME SCENE - ELBERT PRACTICE FIELD - LATER

where much of The Block dehydrates along with Will.

NARRATOR (V.O.)

The week before classes that year broke all records for heat. It got to the point that if it had dropped below 100 degrees...

Will tries to lift his head to the sun, but can't.

NARRATOR (V.O.)

...we would've huddled for warmth. We needn't have worried, though. For some thoughtful University committee had provided us a practice field with the most anti-reflective, sun-sucking surface known to man...

Will pries his horn out of Elbert Practice Field, leaving a distinct impression in the

NARRATOR (V.O.)

...tar. Resting too long put us in danger of becoming the world's largest Roach Motel: "They march in, but they don't march out..."

DRUM MAJOR

Everybody <u>up</u>!

MMB

One...

NARRATOR (V.O.)

'Happily', that never became a problem...

TWEET! TWEET! TWEET! TWEET!

MMB

Up.

(beat-beat)

Lock.

Another SWEEP, but much faster than before. Will's struggle begins immediately.

NARRATOR (V.O.)

Still, even with "The Lock" and the heat and the tar and the sweeps, I might have survived "Hell Week" unscathed if it hadn't been for the Prince of Marching Darkness...

Marko suddenly appears at Will's side:

NARRATOR (V.O.)

Marko-stopheles.

Marko matches Will stride-for-stride.

MARKO

Come on, where's the lock, <u>where's</u> the lock?

NARRATOR (V.O.)

Yes, under the ever watchful thighs of Marko...

MARKO

Lock it, <u>lock</u> it...!

NARRATOR (V.O.)

...my purgatory was complete.

MARKO

Lock, lock, lock, lock...!

And as Will suffers heat both physical and verbal

CUT TO:

SAME SCENE - MUCH LATER - EARLY EVENING

where Will stands at attention, still PANTING.

NARRATOR (V.O.)

But even Hell has a timeclock...

DRUM MAJOR

Eight A.M.! Tomorrow morning! Ready to go. Ba-annnd dismissed!

The Block falls out.

THOR

See ya tomorrow, Will. And don't worry, it gets easier.

CHARLIE

Why do you lie to our boy...?

Will almost grins as his rank-mates depart.

NARRATOR (V.O.)

Well, even if it didn't get any easier, I figured I could lapse into a lock-induced coma and have about 12 full hours to recover...

Will starts stiffly toward the gate, but is recalled by

MARKO

(t)odd!

and an ominously beckoning finger.

NARRATOR (V.O.)
...or 12 full seconds, as it turned out.

Marko leads Will to the sideline, where several familiar trumpets await.

NARRATOR (V.O.)
It was only then that I found out why all those trumpets below Chair Number 75 had stuck around.

Will joins a Noah-line being organized by the Drum Major, instruments gathered two-by-two.

NARRATOR (V.O.)
They were called "Reserves", and were kept on the sidelines to fill in whenever a hole appeared in The Block due to absence or illness.

Will finds himself second in line, behind another pair of trumpets.

NARRATOR (V.O.)
Every Reserve had the right to "Challenge" into The Block at the end of practice.

The first pair of trumpets are led out to a yardline. There's something very "gladiatorial" about the whole thing.

NARRATOR (V.O.)
This required each rank to put one of its members up for Challenge - a choice made by the Rank Leader.

Will sees Marko kidding around with the Rank 9 Leader, whose own member is now up on the line.

NARRATOR (V.O.)
And for the first time, I got an idea of how I had made Rank 8...

Will looks beyond the fence, where secure members of The Block smile and laugh on their way back to Reveille Hall.

But his attention is snapped back to the field by FOUR SHARP WHISTLES, an "Up!", a "Lock!", and the first pair of trumpets marching down the lined asphalt.

NARRATOR (V.O.)

It was a simple test with three judges: The Drum Major, a Graduate Assistant - or "grad ass" as they were affectionately known...

The Drum Major and a bearded twentysomething in band jacket parallel the pair down the field - the GRAD ASS stumbling.

NARRATOR (V.O.)

...and a wild card depending on the particular instrument being challenged - namely...

Another WHISTLE, a "Drop!", and the two trumpets face their third judge:

NARRATOR (V.O.)

The Section Leader.

Marko. He quickly confers with the other two judges and sends the victor off smiling with the Rank 9 Leader.

DRUM MAJOR

Next pair!

Marko looks up and stops smiling. Will steps to the line.

NARRATOR (V.O.)

It was like trying to skate in front of the Russian judge after an entire day of...

TWEET! TWEET! TWEET! TWEET!

RESERVE #1

Up!

(beat-beat)

Lock!

The sudden start of the Challenge takes Will so much by surprise that he neglects to yell the preparatory beats. However, hours of Locking have conditioned a Pavlovian knee response, and he manages to take off in step.

NARRATOR (V.O.)

Ten yards - sixteen steps in the fading light - was all it took to strangle any small confidence I might have nurtured that day...

Indeed, it's not just fatigue that seems to be darkening Will's face...

...and a TWEET!, "Drop!", and a final step fail to brighten it.

NARRATOR (V.O.)

I don't think I ever even saw the other guy. Or the vote...

Perhaps noticing the look on Will's face, the Drum Major steps over to speak in private:

DRUM MAJOR

(to Will)

You won. See you tomorrow - same time, same place, okay?

Will nods blankly and heads for the gate.

NARRATOR (V.O.)

...which did little to console me. For as I walked back to spend my first night alone in an empty dorm, I realized that even though I had kept my place in The Block...

Will sees the rest of the band, well ahead of him.

NARRATOR (V.O.)

..."home" was still very far away.

And as Will continues to walk alone

DISSOLVE TO:

INT. REVEILLE MUSIC HALL - DAY

CLOSE ON THE SIGN "Fire Up! It's..."

now completed with the word "Tuesday.

THREE NOTES - one long, two short - boom throughout the hall, followed by

CAVENDISH (O.S.)

Again.

The pattern repeats: THREE NOTES and

CAVENDISH (O.S.)

Again.

NARRATOR (V.O.)

At least we were tearing along in the music department.

Will watches Cavendish conduct the same THREE NOTES, give a cut-off, and again announce

CAVENDISH

Again.

NARRATOR (V.O.)

While waiting for the cool of the morning to pass before we headed out to the tar...

THREE NOTES.

CAVENDISH

Again.

NARRATOR (V.O.)

...we spent our entire second rehearsal perfecting the first three notes of our fight song, "The Victors".

THREE NOTES.

CAVENDISH

Again.

NARRATOR (V.O.)

At this rate, we'd be ready to perform our full program...

THREE NOTES.

CAVENDISH

Again.

NARRATOR (V.O.)

...about the time scholarship athletes started walking erect.

THREE NOTES.

CAVENDISH

Again.

NARRATOR (V.O.)

But even with our first game only four days away, I still had more important things to worry about.

Will glances at the Reserve trumpets below him.

THREE NOTES.

NARRATOR (V.O.)

After all, I now knew what was waiting for me at the end of the day...

This time, Cavendish actually looks in Will's direction.

CAVENDISH

Again.

NARRATOR (V.O.)
And the day itself wasn't going to help any...

PRE-LAP

FOUR EXTREMELY FAST WHISTLES which precipitate a

CUT TO:

CLOSE UP - WILL'S FACE

eyes flying wide in shock as

HIS LEFT LEG LOCKS

and all hell breaks loose on

EXT. ELBERT PRACTICE FIELD - DAY

where the PERCUSSION EXPLODES and the entire band double-times in place along the far sideline.

Legs pump. Lungs steam. Sweat glands threaten to unionize.

NARRATOR (V.O.)
Let me try and explain what's happening here. In a word...

ON WILL, suffering:

NARRATOR (V.O.)
Aggghhhhh...!

Now in shorts, his pale legs struggle to keep up with Thor and Charlie, packed fore and aft in single file.

NARRATOR (V.O.)
Well, okay, technically, there was another word. "Pregame."

MMB

Aggghhhhh...!

Split in half, the band begins double-timing onto the field like two giant millipedes scurrying across the asphalt.

NARRATOR (V.O.)

A lot of people think Halftime is the most important time for a marching band. They're wrong. A signature Pregame that drives crowd anticipation to a frenzy is the *true* hallmark of a great college band. And at Michigan...

Will finally takes off from the sideline, but can only muster a FEEBLE YELL.

NARRATOR (V.O.)

...Pregame hadn't changed in over 50 years. It started with a double-time entry...

A ROLL-OUT dissolves the entry lines and all movement suddenly freezes in an "Up!"

NARRATOR (V.O.)

...followed by a fan-out to solid block "M" formation, so that just as everyone had reached the depths of exhaustion...

High atop a specially-build tower, Cavendish throws a massive downbeat to the GASPING band:

NARRATOR (V.O.)

...the show could begin.

The band begins SINGING the "M Fanfare".

NARRATOR (V.O.)

Now, since we didn't all know the music yet, we sang it instead - which is considerably easier than playing...

Though hard to prove by Will - who struggles to SING even his 3rd trumpet part between GASPS.

NARRATOR (V.O.)
...which is considerably easier than...

Cavendish cut everyone off and skips ahead to cue the

CAVENDISH
Last note!

MMB
Laaaaa...!
(beat)
Lock! Daaa, da-da daaa, da-da da, da - da - go...!

NARRATOR (V.O.)
...this.

The band forms back into entry lines and steps off.

NARRATOR (V.O.)
This was the part of Pregame where we swept toward the student endzone while blaring the Intro to "The Victors" - at least three notes of which we could've actually played...

Will is really GULPING FOR AIR now.

NARRATOR (V.O.)
...at least in theory. Right now, though, I'd like to recite a poem I composed on the way downfield. It's called... "Oxygen".
(CLEARS THROAT)
"Oxygen! Oxygen! I need more oxygen! Oh, god - oxygen! Ox-y-geeeeen!" Thank you.

The band turns around and SINGS "The Victors" chorus.

NARRATOR (V.O.)
But it wasn't until we formed the traditional floating block "M" and headed back up the field that things got a bit...

MARKO
(now at Will's side)
Where's the lock? Where's the lock?

NARRATOR (V.O.)
...demanding. Especially when Marko hinted at a personal credo:

MARKO
(in Will's ear)
I wanna hear every note! Every note! This is Rank 8! We play every note! Every note!

NARRATOR (V.O.)
Now, I couldn't have played every note if I were sitting down. And actually playing. As it was...

Will's trumpet bobs uncontrollably in front of his face.

NARRATOR (V.O.)
I'd be lucky if I didn't 'mouthpiece' an eye out.
(beat)
But I tried to at least sing as many notes through the rest of Pregame as voluntary asphyxiation would allow. Through "The Victors"...

And as Will tries to keep up with Marko

SAME SCENE - MINUTES LATER

NARRATOR (V.O.)
Through the opposing team's fight song...

SAME SCENE - MINUTES LATER

NARRATOR (V.O.)
Through the "Star Spangled Banner"...

SAME SCENE - MINUTES LATER

NARRATOR (V.O.)
Through a final chorus of "The Victors" to get us off the field...

The band TAGS "The Victors" and begins double-timing again on the near sideline.

Will can barely lift his legs.

NARRATOR (V.O.)
Through a silent prayer for swift and merciful death.

The CADENCE ENDS and a CHEER goes up. Pregame is over. Will lifts his head in relief:

NARRATOR (V.O.)
It was like the answer to my prayers...

CAVENDISH
(from tower)
Again!

NARRATOR (V.O.)
...except for the "swift and merciful" part.

And as Will peers heavenward at the tower while the rest of the band scrambles across the field

CUT TO:

SAME SCENE - MUCH LATER - EARLY EVENING

where Will, visibly drained, stands on the line next to a trumpet Reserve.

NARRATOR (V.O.)
By the end of the day, when I was put up for the inevitable Challenge, I thought about committing Block Suicide. I could end this right here, right now.

The Drum Major blows FOUR WHISTLES:

RESERVE #2
Up!
(beat-beat)
Lock!

Will takes off down the field.

NARRATOR (V.O.)
But sometimes nature conspires against you.

Will looks at his challenger - god's gift to incoordination.

NARRATOR (V.O.)
The Reserve I was up against looked like he was marching to an AA meeting.

They stop. The judges don't take long.

NARRATOR (V.O.)
I won the Challenge. I'd be back again tomorrow...

On his way off the field, Will catches Marko's glare.

NARRATOR (V.O.)
...to do it all over again.

And as Will limps toward the gate

DISSOLVE TO:

INT. REVEILLE MUSIC HALL - DAY

CLOSE ON THE SIGN: "Fire Up! It's..."

now completed with the word "Wednesday".

NARRATOR (V.O.)
It's come time for an ugly confession. I put it off as long as possible, but can't anymore.

The band waits patiently while Cavendish examines his music.

NARRATOR (V.O.)
This is a period piece. I went to college years ago, but the story's being told in a contemporary setting because it's a lot cheaper to do that way.

Satisfied, Cavendish readies his baton.

NARRATOR (V.O.)
Why tell you now? Well, because the next morning, we actually started rehearsing the music for our Halftime show. And in keeping with my promise of truth...

CAVENDISH
Let's take it from "D"-Daddy-Dog...

Off his downbeat, the band plunges into

THE ANTHEM OF A GENERATION

the "ah-ah-ah-ah" bolstered by a CRESCENDOING SNARE that DETONATES the PERCUSSION SECTION along with the full force of the BAND in a blood-curdling

"Stayin' Aliiiiiiiiiiiiiiiiiiiiiiiiiiiiiiiiiiiiiiiiiiiiiive!"

seemingly without end.

It's Disco. Marching band style.

Will actually rolls his eyes:

NARRATOR (V.O.)
I weep for my generation.

The FUNKINESS continues.

NARRATOR (V.O.)
Fortunately, the morning also delivered something infinitely cooler...

CUT TO:

INT. REVEILLE HALLWAY OF LOCKERS

where Will stands wearing one of the newly assigned - but debatably "cooler" - marching band

NARRATOR (V.O.)
Uniforms.

Will smiles while checking the fit. Others around him do the same.

NARRATOR (V.O.)
Since I was in The Block, I got the full workup:
Spats, gloves, cords, hat...

Will takes a stiff, boxy hat out of his locker, along with a long cardboard tube.

NARRATOR (V.O.)
...and the crowning glory itself...
(from tube)
...a plume.

Will rams the tall feathered column into the front of his hat and tries it on.

NARRATOR (V.O.)
I know, I know - there's something militantly goofy about the whole thing. But with this baby on...

Will examines himself in a mirror.

NARRATOR (V.O.)
...you literally were seven feet tall.

Will turns sideways in the mirror.

NARRATOR (V.O.)
I could feel the week turning around. And sure enough...

And as Will lifts his uniformed leg in The Lock, FRAMING DOWN to approximate the recruitment poster he once saw in C.R.I.S.P.

CUT TO:

EXT. ELBERT PRACTICE FIELD - (THAT) DAY

where Will's now bare white leg accompanies an entire rank of leisurely Locks:

NARRATOR (V.O.)
...practice that day was easier.

THE SHOT WIDENS to include Rank 8 "hand-jiving" in precise unison while accompanied by an equally FUNKY DRUM CADENCE. It's a textbook Marching Band Disco Entry.

NARRATOR (V.O.)
Sillier, but easier.

Indeed, Will and several of his rank-mates are actually smiling.

NARRATOR (V.O.)
We concentrated on putting steps to music for our Halftime show.

CHARLIE
I am wondering if people will even recall Rock-N-Roll ten years from now.

THOR
What are you talking about?

CHARLIE
Face it, please - Disco is here to stay.

NARRATOR (V.O.)
Charlie was an economics major.

Thor looks back and grins at Will. Their hand-jives intensi-funk.

NARRATOR (V.O.)
And even better, near the end of practice, I got to sit back, relax...

CUT TO:

SAME SCENE - LATER

where Will sits back on the grassy sideline with the rest of the band and looks at three figures, including Guy, who stand at attention with whistles around their necks:

NARRATOR (V.O.)
...and pass judgement on others for a change.

TWEEET! It comes from

FIGURE #1
Double command! Ten-hut! Ten-hut! One, two, three!

He executes a standard 3-step attention, a little rushed.

NARRATOR (V.O.)
The occasion was Drum Major tryouts. And even though Guy had held the job for the past two years and was a virtual shoo-in, he still had to go through the motions.

TWEEEEET!

DRUM MAJOR (GUY)

Double command! Ten-hut! Ten-hut! One! Two! Three!

Three perfect Locks.

MMB

Ooooooo...

NARRATOR (V.O.)

But the one guy that got me was the last guy.

FWOOO...! FWOOO...!

FIGURE #3 seems to be having trouble with his whistle. Slight and prematurely balding, he abandons his bird call and precedes in an odd, modulated, trans-Anglo accent:

FIGURE #3

Dupple commaaaaand! A-teeen-shut! A-teeen-shut! One...! Two...! Three...!

Holding each Lock a hair too long, feet flat, it's possible his whistle was a duck call after all.

Will can barely contain a snicker.

NARRATOR (V.O.)

And even before the inevitable vote for Guy...

SNICKER containment fails.

NARRATOR (V.O.)

...I no longer felt like the band's biggest loser.

Will is not alone in his assessment of Figure #3.

NARRATOR (V.O.)

But the best part of it was...

And as Figure #3 holds his baton in stiff, Grenadierian attention, ignoring the SNICKERS

CUT TO:

SAME SCENE - LATER - EARLY EVENING

where Will strides alongside another trumpet Reserve:

NARRATOR (V.O.)
...I was able to carry that feeling into my next Challenge.

WILL & RESERVE
And - drop!

They drop their horns and stand at attention. The judges confer.

NARRATOR (V.O.)
And you know what happened?

Guy steps over with a look of sympathy.

DRUM MAJOR
I'm sorry...
(turns to Will)
Good job, Will. See you tomorrow.

NARRATOR (V.O.)
I won. Now I'll bet a lot of you thought there was gonna be a typical movie reversal there and I was gonna lose. Admit it.

Will heads for the gate, smiling.

NARRATOR (V.O.)
Well, the truth is, a little confidence is the best weapon you can carry into a challenge.

Beyond the gate, Will hustles to catch up with the rest of The Block.

NARRATOR (V.O.)
I had gone from fearing yesterday, to actually looking forward to...

CUT TO:

THE SIGN "Fire Up! It's..."

now completed with the word "Thursday".

NARRATOR (V.O.)
...tomorrow. And while I'm in this good mood, it's time for a rather large digression - namely...

CUT TO:

ANOTHER SIGN

this one a small rectangle with the single word "Women":

NARRATOR (V.O.)
...girls.

The sign swings back with its door as a young woman enters the Ladies Room off of

INT. REVEILLE HALLWAY OF LOCKERS - DAY

where Will takes note while assembling his trumpet.

NARRATOR (V.O.)
We had 'em. I didn't. End of digression.

Will SHUTS his case.

NARRATOR (V.O.)
Actually, it's not quite that simple. And since every movie is required by law to have some sort of romance - no matter how obscure...

Will SLAMS his locker.

NARRATOR (V.O.)
...I'll go into it here. Let's start with some basic facts...

Will starts down the hallway, passing other males assembling their instruments.

NARRATOR (V.O.)
There was a time not too long ago when marching bands didn't allow girls. But this was the enlightened Age of Disco...

Will now passes a few Farrah-clones, one with a tight "Afternoon Delight" T-shirt. He tries not to stare.

NARRATOR (V.O.)
...and the MMB was enlightened more than most because we believed in something called "Blend". See, most marching bands are predominantly...

Will opens the door and enters

THE MAIN REHEARSAL HALL

encountering a WALL OF WARM-UP SOUND:

NARRATOR (V.O.)
...loud. And loud means predominantly brass and brass means predominantly...

Will looks at the Tuba and Trombone Sections, virtually all

NARRATOR (V.O.)
...male. For even in this enlightened age, there was a distinct segregation of the sexes by instrument.

Will turns to the all-male Percussion Section, beating on their instruments like in the Elementary School Flashback.

NARRATOR (V.O.)

But since the MMB preferred a more orchestral blend, we also included a number of the softer, but "fairer", instruments.

Will starts a long circuit to the front of the room.

NARRATOR (V.O.)

Here they are by Section. Clarinets...

ON THE CLARINET SECTION

90% female:

NARRATOR (V.O.)

...one of the womanly woodwind family, with the occasional mama's boy thrown in for good measure. But in terms of highest overall femininity, the reigning rank was definitely the Pics...

ON THE PICCOLO SECTION

100% female, with two of its members warming up to the FLUTE DUET from "Dance of the Sugar Plum Fairy".

NARRATOR (V.O.)

"Woe to any man with a fife, for he shall be outcasteth amongst his brethren."

Now at the front of the room, Will gets in line for an automatic tuning machine, flipping through his valves.

NARRATOR (V.O.)

As for my own highly masculine instrument, we did get the occasional valve-crasher. These came in two types: The Butch and The Beautiful. Out of 75 trumpets, we had one of each.

ON THE TRUMPET SECTION

where a girl who could make Bela Abzug wince practices the theme from "Rocky", the guy next to her involuntarily leaning away.

NARRATOR (V.O.)
Fortunately, The Butch was far removed, in the firsts, where she had something to prove.
(beat)
Unfortunately, The Beautiful was also far removed, in the seconds...

Will steps up to the tuner, but keeps an eye on the nearest chair at the end of one of the trumpet rows:

NARRATOR (V.O.)
...where she had nothing more she *could* prove.

REVEAL THE BEAUTIFUL - a deeply tanned and toned girl with long brown hair and "this better be good" eyes.

NARRATOR (V.O.)
In an era before health clubs, her body would've made The Hulk wanna throw on a T-shirt.

Will plays his tuning note, adjusts his slide, and tries again - all while using just one eye.

NARRATOR (V.O.)
And god only knew what she could do with that embouchure. All in all, it made for...

Will continues adjusting his slide at the machine - the long all-male line behind him in no particular hurry.

NARRATOR (V.O.)
...a very well-tuned ensemble. But the real lottery winner of The Block...

CUT TO:

EXT. ELBERT PRACTICE FIELD - (LATER THAT) DAY

where an overheating male trumpet stands at attention with eyes glued forward:

NARRATOR (V.O.)
...was the guy who got to march behind her all season.

FOUR WHISTLES initiate a lift and hold, the perspiring trumpet grimacing in discomfort.

NARRATOR (V.O.)
Although he did occasionally give new meaning to "The Lock".

Will notices the drama from the corner of his eye, then drops his own leg after a WHISTLE and an

DRUM MAJOR (O.S.)
At ease...

NARRATOR (V.O.)
But as far as I was concerned, there was only *one* Section in the marching band for girls.

Will leans to one side to better peer upfield.

NARRATOR (V.O.)
They practiced slightly apart from The Block, by themselves.

Will spots a corps of girls in casual congregation at the edge of the asphalt.

NARRATOR (V.O.)
They were distant, special...

And as Will's eyes widen a bit

CLOSE ON ONE OF THE GIRLS lifting a bare leg to tie her shoe, an act which an 18-year-old boy just might find

NARRATOR (V.O.)
(throaty)
...exotic.

She returns to her peers - a healthy, if mostly representative, group of young college women.

NARRATOR (V.O.)
They either didn't play an instrument or couldn't get into The Block with the one they did play - and hence had been deepened by a tragic element.

They girls form up into two full ranks, crouching down for something.

NARRATOR (V.O.)
They were mysterious. They had secrets. They had...

SNAP! The corps bolts to attention with billowing

NARRATOR (V.O.)
...flags.

BACK ON WILL, enraptured.

NARRATOR (V.O.)
But there was one flag in particular that stood apart...

Like the sea before Moses, The Block in front of Will begins to part:

NARRATOR (V.O.)
She was the most perfect girl in the entire corps...

THE SHOT TRACKS FORWARD through the ranks:

NARRATOR (V.O.)
The flag de la flag...

The final, frontmost rank parts, leaving...

NARRATOR (V.O.)
Jeannie Winterspoon.

...BATHED IN WHITE LIGHT that paints a halo of her blond hair as the ANGELS SING

ANGELS (V.O.)
Ah-ahhh...

and the SHOT TIGHTENS:

NARRATOR (V.O.)
She was Grace Kelly in marching shorts. An eastern debutante lost in the Midwest on the way to the ball. She was...

RESUME ON WILL

as The Block reappears before him with the sound of a heavy metal door CLANGING SHUT:

NARRATOR (V.O.)
...totally unobtainable.

Will shuffles his feet as the rest of the band continues their "at ease" lull.

NARRATOR (V.O.)
Jeannie Winterspoon was more than just eight ranks away. She was like a star whose light could only be perceived across vast, silent expanses of time. A celestial body...
(as Will peeks)
...with *great* legs.

Will continues to bob and lean to keep a clear eyeline.

NARRATOR (V.O.)
The question was, how could a boy defy the laws of physics, and approach the sun without getting burned?

DRUM MAJOR

Water!

And as The Block disperses for a water break

SAME SCENE - MINUTES LATER

where band members cluster around several water stations set up along the sideline, each consisting of a cooler on a chair, and a trash can for empty paper cups.

Will approaches one of these coolers with an empty cup. But just as he reaches for the tap, his cup collides with the cup of

JEANNIE WINTERSPOON

Oh, pardon me.

WILL

No, no - please.

JEANNIE WINTERSPOON

Oh, I couldn't.

WILL

But I insist.

JEANNIE WINTERSPOON

Thank you.

She places her cup under the tap. Will reaches for the handle:

WILL

Allow me.

Hands meet. Eyes follow. And the sound of water DRIBBLING SWELLS WITH

THE THEME FROM "ROMEO AND JULIET"

just like a "love at first sight" movie encounter - except this one is played exclusively by

A SOLO TUBA

who ROTATES INTO VIEW behind them.

RESUME ON WILL

back in The Block "at ease":

NARRATOR (V.O.)
Oh, all right, it's not true. With a girl like Jeannie Winterspoon, there was only one way this could go...

DRUM MAJOR
Water!

BACK ON THE SIDELINES - MINUTES LATER

as Will's cup reaches for the tap and again bumps into

JEANNIE WINTERSPOON
Oh, I'm sorry.

WILL
No, no - it's okay.

Their eyes meet. And hold. The tension is growing palpable. Then:

JEANNIE WINTERSPOON
I have a boyfriend on the football team.

RESUME ON WILL

back in The Block:

NARRATOR (V.O.)
Okay, not true, either. But I felt I had to give you a couple of movie extremes to bound a reality you might not like...

DRUM MAJOR

Water!

BACK ON THE SIDELINES - MINUTES LATER

as Will looks up from another cup bump to see...

JEANNIE WINTERSPOON

Oh...

...whom he motions to continue without saying a word. She fills her cup...

...and walks away.

NARRATOR (V.O.)

That was it. Nothing more. And you know what?

RESUME ON WILL

for the last time:

NARRATOR (V.O.)

Even *that's* an exaggeration.

DRUM MAJOR

Water!

Will disperses with the rest of The Block toward the sideline.

NARRATOR (V.O.)

The truth is the boy never even got close to Jeannie Winterspoon. Never even heard the sound of her voice. Never even tried.

Will fills his cup at a water station. Jeannie Winterspoon is nowhere in sight.

He crumples the cup and throws it away.

NARRATOR (V.O.)
So much for romance.

Will heads back to the asphalt.

NARRATOR (V.O.)
Now some of you may be wondering why the heck I brought this up in the first place if nothing happened. "Damn depressing, Todd." Yeah, well...
(beat)
...something did happen. But not for a long time...

Will takes up his Block position on the nearly empty field.

NARRATOR (V.O.)
I promise I'll tie it all in by the time we get to the end of the story. But for now...

Will looks down at the asphalt.

NARRATOR (V.O.)
I had other challenges to face.

And as Will positions his arches on the yardline

MATCH CUT TO:

SAME SCENE - MUCH LATER - EARLY EVENING

where Will again positions his arches on a yardline - this time next to another TRUMPET RESERVE:

NARRATOR (V.O.)
But the day had gone pretty well again, and I was beginning to think that maybe, just maybe - someday - there might be...

Will turns to see a graduate assistant wearing

NARRATOR (V.O.)
...a band jacket with my name on it.

TWEET! TWEET! TWEET! TWEET!

WILL & TRUMPET RESERVE

Up!

(beat-beat)

Lock!

They both step off down the field, Marko and the Drum Major waiting. But Will keeps one eye on the sideline, where the band jacket follows along:

NARRATOR (V.O.)

Now nobody would've been caught dead wearing a band jacket in high school. But here it was different. They were a coat of honor, patches down the sleeve bearing testament to Veterans of Foreign Bowl Games.

Will and the Trumpet Reserve lock side-by-side.

NARRATOR (V.O.)

Who knew what faraway locales might grace my own sleeve someday? It filled me with a feeling of...

CLOSE ON - WILL'S FOOT

overstepping the yardline as the Challenge concludes:

NARRATOR (V.O.)

...pride.

The judges confer.

NARRATOR (V.O.)

I know what you're thinking: "Pride goeth before a fall." You're expecting another one of those movie reversals where just when you thought I was getting the hang of this stuff, I lose, aren't you? Well...

The Drum Major steps over. He looks at both trumpets.

NARRATOR (V.O.)

...you're right.

DRUM MAJOR

(to Reserve)

You're now Block Number 82. Report in the morning.

(turning)

I'm sorry, Will.

Automatically, Will turns and leaves the field.

NARRATOR (V.O.)

That's what really happened. I lost the Challenge. I lost my place in The Block. But it wasn't until...

CUT TO:

THE SIGN "Fire Up! It's..."

now completed with the word "Friday".

NARRATOR (V.O.)

...that I realized just how much I had lost.

An excited BUZZ fills the

MAIN REHEARSAL HALL

as people mill about before the start of practice:

NARRATOR (V.O.)

Friday was the day the entire band had been looking forward to - the day we rehearsed beyond the hot-tarred familiarity of our practice field, to the cool-grassed sacristy of...

CUT TO:

A MIGHTY SIGN that reads "MICHIGAN STADIUM":

NARRATOR (V.O.)
...the largest college football stadium in the land.

EXT. MICHIGAN STADIUM - DAY

where The Block, reverent, stands in a parking lot outside the massive entrance tunnel.

NARRATOR (V.O.)
Though I had grown up watching the games on TV, I had never actually stepped inside Michigan Stadium before.

THE SHOT TRACKS PAST THE BLOCK, lingering at a Will-less Rank 8 before continuing rapidly toward the back:

NARRATOR (V.O.)
Now, on the threshold of that moment, I came not as one of the anointed, but as one of the...

GRAD ASS
Reserves!

At the very back of The Block, a single rank falls out. They carry equipment rather than instruments.

The Graduate Assistant - who finally submits to the heat and abandons his band jacket on a pile of boxes - waves the solemn group forward.

Will is among them, shouldering his ladder like a cross.

NARRATOR (V.O.)
I was a leper - one of the untouchables...

Indeed, as the Reserves file past, many in The Block avert their eyes.

NARRATOR (V.O.)
I felt less like I was entering a stadium...

And as Will enters the tunnel

INT. MICHIGAN STADIUM

as he emerges onto 100,000 empty seats:

NARRATOR (V.O.)
...than a symbol of my future with the band.

Will carries his ladder toward the edge of the field.

NARRATOR (V.O.)
The sky may have been clear...

GRAD ASS
No, no - go *around* the field.

NARRATOR (V.O.)
...but a storm was brewing nevertheless.

Robbed of his chance to even step onto the field, a darkening Will carries his ladder back toward the side of the tunnel.

NARRATOR (V.O.)
And then the thunder exploded.

FOUR FAINT WHISTLES drift from the tunnel, followed by

AN EXPLOSION OF DRUMS

THUNDERING THE ENTRY CADENCE as The Block pours forth and SCREAMS onto the field.

Will can only watch, helpless, as the band BLURS past him:

NARRATOR
They took possession of the field like it was theirs.
Like they belonged...

Will turns away and places his ladder against a wall.

NARRATOR (V.O.)

But that way was lost to me. And couldn't be recovered - because Challenges weren't allowed again until Monday.

GRAD ASS

Reserves!

Will joins the other Reserves around the Grad Ass, who INSTRUCTS them from a portable podium on the sideline.

NARRATOR (V.O.)

Instead, I listened to how I'd be spending Saturday - Game Day - holding ladders, hauling equipment, and especially...

GRAD ASS

Apples - go!

He hits a stopwatch and the Reserves hustle back to the tunnel.

NARRATOR (V.O.)

...fetching boxes of fruit at Halftime for the nourishment of the worthy.

The other Reserves reenter the tunnel, but Will pauses a moment to look back at the band, now spread across the field.

NARRATOR (V.O.)

And that's when I got the idea.

Will disappears into the tunnel even as the first Reserves are reemerging with empty apple boxes between them. More and more return...

...but Will is not among them. And when it becomes apparent that something is wrong

EXT. MICHIGAN STADIUM

as Will leaves the darkened tunnel, walking away:

NARRATOR (V.O.)

I got as far as the parking lot before I paused.

Eyes still fixed ahead, Will just stops.

NARRATOR (V.O.)

I know it may not seem like much to you sitting there - a kid about to quit band, so what?

Will appears increasingly troubled.

NARRATOR (V.O.)

But there are times in your life when you realize that no matter how mundane the decision is you're about to make, it's going to color everything you do from that point forward.

Will's eyes don't waver.

NARRATOR (V.O.)

I was at that point. This really was one of the hardest decisions I ever had to make. The Big Quit. And you know what tipped the scales? Get ready, because this is getting close to being an actual movie moment here...

Will's eyes finally move - and light upon

THE BAND JACKET

left behind on some boxes by the Grad Ass.

NARRATOR (V.O.)

The damn jacket. That's right. And the damn patches that went with it. This little trivial piece of... *wool*-in-the-middle-of-a-heat-wave was actually giving me pause.

Will lifts the sleeve and runs his fingers over the patches.

NARRATOR (V.O.)

But was it trivial? Is anything that helps you make a decision like this trivial? I don't know. All I know is...

Will drops the sleeve.

NARRATOR (V.O.)

...I went back inside the tunnel.

(beat)

Even though I couldn't see any light at the end...

And as he disappears into its darkness

DISSOLVE TO:

TITLE CARD: "ACT THREE: Game Day"

CUT TO:

EXT. ELBERT PRACTICE FIELD - MORNING

where the band stretches before the start of final practice in shorts, T-shirts - and plumed band hats.

NARRATOR (V.O.)

I'd like to say things immediately improved after I made that decision...

A BANDSMAN walks by with fist thrust in the air...

BANDSMAN

Fire up! It's Saturday!

...passing a gloomy Will along the sideline:

NARRATOR (V.O.)

...but they didn't.

Will and several other Reserves police the area for litter.

NARRATOR (V.O.)

Reserves were subject to a number of unique humiliations on game day - though so far, I had been spared the worst.

GRAD ASS (O.S.)

Todd!

Will winces, then crosses the field toward the Grad Ass.

NARRATOR (V.O.)

Like drones in a hive, our only mandate was to serve The Block.

Will arrives at the edge of The Block, where the Grad Ass waits with a piccolo whose plume is bent.

NARRATOR (V.O.)

And so, on the morning of my first big day in college...

Will stands immobile as the Grad Ass YANKS the plume from his hat.

NARRATOR (V.O.)

...I was deplumed.

The Grad Ass then cleverly places the piccolo's broken plume in Will's hat and sends him back to litter patrol with a

GRAD ASS

Dismissed.

Will drags back toward the sideline with plume at half mast.

NARRATOR (V.O.)

I had now hit both the figurative *and* literal low point of MMB...

DRUM MAJOR (O.S.)

Todd!

Maybe not, for Will winces even harder at this second call:

NARRATOR (V.O.)
What? What'd they want from me now? A *kidney?*

But the wince is nothing compared to the turn - where Will sees the Drum Major beckoning him toward a very stern-faced Marko:

NARRATOR (V.O.)
Great - a summons from Trumpet Valhalla. It would probably take Odin himself to pull me out of this one...

TRUMPET
(to friend as they pass)
Hey, did you hear about Thor's father...?

Will stops a moment to examine The Block:

NARRATOR (V.O.)
Come to think of it, where *was* Thor...?

MARKO
(t)<u>odd</u>!

Will hurries over to his former Rank Leader. The Drum Major speaks quietly:

DRUM MAJOR
Will, listen - Thor's dad had a heart attack.

NARRATOR (V.O.)
Now, just so this doesn't turn tragic, I'll use the mandatory respectful pause here to tell you that Thor's dad made a full recovery.

WILL
When?

DRUM MAJOR

Last night. We need you to march in his spot - 81.

MARKO

(under his breath)

There are more *senior* Reserves.

DRUM MAJOR

He marched right next to his spot for an entire week, now lay off, Marko.

The retort is not lost on Will, who begins to get a sense that someone may have taken note of his plight after all.

Marko raises his arms in biblical resignation and walks off.

DRUM MAJOR

(to Will)

Come on...

NARRATOR (V.O.)

And just like that, I was back in The Block. I was going to march on game day after all. I was going to march in Michigan Stadium in front of 100,000 screaming fans...

The Drum Major places Will in Block Position 81:

NARRATOR (V.O.)

...right - next - to Marko.

It's true. Will now stands directly next to the scowling Rank Leader, who immediately abandons the proximity and steps forward:

MARKO

All right, Rank 8, listen up!

(prowling)

This is *Saturday*. *Game* Day. *No excuses day*. There are only three things you need to remember today. One: You will Lock on every step! *Every* step! I had better not have to ask even one person, *one person* 'Where's The Lock?' today - this is Game Day - we Lock on every step! And on every step you will play every note! That's Two: *Every* note! This is Rank 8! *My* rank! I play every note - you will play every note! <u>Every</u> - <u>note</u>!"

Marko doesn't bother to add Will's name, opting instead to sear-stare directly into his face.

The Drum Major counters in a lower voice:

DRUM MAJOR

Don't worry about playing. Just concentrate on learning the new position, okay?

Having done what he could, the Drum Major pats Will's shoulder and moves away.

TRUMPET (O.S.)

Hey, Marko, what about "Three"?

MARKO

Three...

(whispers into Will's ear)

I'm your judge.

Marko finally returns to the head of Rank 8.

NARRATOR (V.O.)

Kickoff was at 12:00. High noon.

(beat)

Like it or not, I was back in the game...

And as Will stands at rigid attention

CUT TO:

EXT. REVEILLE MUSIC HALL - DAY

where Will, still at rigid attention, involuntarily flinches as a plume is RAMMED back into his hat:

NARRATOR (V.O.)
...and in <u>full</u> uniform.

Will returns the grin of the now elaborately-costumed Drum Major, who moves down the line...

...to review the rest of The Block, also in full uniform.

NARRATOR (V.O.)
Final inspection was really just a show for the crowds on the way to the stadium. But I was actually starting to enjoy myself - from my fresh straight plume right down to my--

MARKO
Dirty wrinkled spats. Did you polish those?

Uniform pride dissolves as a maize-and-blue mountain of frown now stands before Will.

WILL
Uh, they're... well... they're brand new.

MARKO
That's not what I asked.

He pulls Will's mouthpiece and leers inside - disgusted:

MARKO
You put this in your mouth?

WILL
I used a pipe cleaner to--

MARKO
That's <u>not</u> what I asked.
(replaces it)

Don't worry. You'll have plenty of time to clean up - come Monday.

His meaning is clear. But before Marko can move on:

DRUM MAJOR (O.S.)

I have a better idea.

The Drum Major has been inspecting the rank behind them, but now steps back up next to Will.

MARKO

Do you, Guy?

DRUM MAJOR

Yeah, I do. Marko.

Marko folds his arms magnanimously.

DRUM MAJOR

(to Will)

You've been Challenged all four days this week, haven't you?

WILL

Yeah.

DRUM MAJOR

(for Marko)

That's a lot for one position.

He looks at the Trumpet Reserve in Will's spot.

DRUM MAJOR

And after Thor gets back, there'll be more Challenging for this same position, won't there?

MARKO

So?

DRUM MAJOR
So what if we treat today like the Ultimate Challenge - and whoever performs best gets to have this spot an entire week - no other Challenges allowed?

MARKO
That's not the rules.

DRUM MAJOR
(pointed)
That's not what I asked.

Even Marko knows this is a power struggle he can't win.

MARKO
You're the Drum Major.

DRUM MAJOR
Then it's settled. Guys...
(to Will and Reserve)
...good luck.

He returns to inspecting the rank behind them. Marko looks at the Trumpet Reserve:

MARKO
Don't sweat it. I'm still the Section judge...
(for Will's benefit)
...and I'm *sure* you'll do fine.

Marko continues his own inspection of the rest of Rank 8, leaving Will at attention:

NARRATOR (V.O.)
But with a chance to get my spot back, I decided right then and there...

Will makes a minute adjustment to his horn carry:

NARRATOR (V.O.)
I would out-attention this guy...

CUT TO:

EXT. STREET - LATER

where the trumpet section "camelwalks" in looping strides while the rest of The Block straight-marches:

NARRATOR (V.O.)
I would out-parade this guy...

CUT TO:

INT. TUNNEL - LATER

where the band CHANTS

MMB
Let's go Blue! Let's go Blue...!

while packed tightly in the darkness:

NARRATOR (V.O.)
...and I would out-tunnel this guy.

Will and the Trumpet Reserve spy each other and CHANT with renewed vigor.

NARRATOR (V.O.)
With Pregame only minutes away, I was firing up for The Ultimate Challenge.
(beat)
But my psyching up was suddenly cut short...

DEAD SILENCE falls on the tunnel as foreign jerseys stream past. Will turns away with the rest of the band.

NARRATOR (V.O.)
...and while the visiting team went back to their locker room, and 250 professional noisemakers fell utterly silent...

One of the visitors tries to raise a YELL, but it falters in the eerie quiet of the darkened tunnel.

NARRATOR (V.O.)
...I began to wonder if I wasn't being psyched out, too.

The threat passes, and the band moves on to another tradition - SINGING the Alma Mater:

MMB
"Sing to the colors,
That float in the light;
Hurrah for The Yellow and Blue."

Not knowing the words, Will can only listen. And reflect:

NARRATOR (V.O.)
I began to wonder what was really happening here.

MMB
"Yellow the stars,
As they ride through the night;
And reel in a rollicking crew."

NARRATOR (V.O.)
What was really important?

MMB
"Yellow the fields,
Where ripens the grain..."

NARRATOR (V.O.)
Maybe I'd been wrong about this whole thing.

MMB
"And yellow the moon,
On the harvest wane - Hail!"

NARRATOR (V.O.)
Maybe I'd been underselling myself this whole time.

MMB

"Hail to the colors,
That float in the light..."

NARRATOR (V.O.)

And maybe the question I really needed to ask was...

MMB

"Hurrah for The Yellow and Blue!"

NARRATOR (V.O.)

Was I Yellow...?

The band resumes its CHANT of

MMB

Let's go Blue! Let's go Blue!

NARRATOR (V.O.)

...or was I Blue?

TWEEEEET!

The band stiffens and faces forward.

PRESSBOX ANNOUNCER (V.O.)

(from field)

Ladieeeees and gentlemen! Introducing the 250 member Mmmmmmichigan Marching Band!

(CROWD NOISE)

Baaaaand...

NARRATOR (V.O.)

And it was only at that moment, finally seeing the light at the end of the tunnel...

PRESSBOX ANNOUNCER (V.O.)

...take the field!

TWEET! TWEET! TWEET! TWEET!

MMB

Hup!

The tunnel SHATTERS in ENTRY CADENCE - Will's eyes unflinching:

NARRATOR (V.O.)

...that I knew what to do.

The Block surges toward the light.

NARRATOR (V.O.)

Instead of the expected...

Will reaches the end of the long, dark passage:

NARRATOR (V.O.)

...I chose to be reborn.

And as Will bursts from the metaphoric tunnel

CUT TO:

INT. MICHIGAN STADIUM

WILL'S P.O.V. - AN EXPLOSION OF SIGHT AND SOUND

as he double-times down a yardline, SCREAMING like a newborn:

NARRATOR (V.O.)

It must've been incredible - the color, the noise... But I was too busy concentrating on something else. And it wasn't the Trumpet Reserve nipping at my heels...

Indeed, when the Entry Line experiences a momentary bunch-up, the Trumpet Reserve nearly climbs Will's back.

NARRATOR (V.O.)

No, it was the <u>ultimate</u> Ultimate Challenge of the Michigan Marching Band...

Will suddenly pulls up directly behind

NARRATOR (V.O.)

Marko.

matching his Rank and Section Leader stride for double stride. In fact, Will's knees pump even higher:

NARRATOR (V.O.)

If he was the best the MMB had to offer, I was going to match him step for step...

Marko raises a fist and SCREAMS. Will raise both fists, horn and all, and SCREAMS with such primal ferocity that Marko actually looks back over his shoulder:

NARRATOR (V.O.)

...and note for note.

Will smiles and continues to pound the turf.

NARRATOR (V.O.)

Screw trying to prove to others that I belonged. I was going to prove it to myself.

(beat)

There was only one problem...

Will's smile fades as he begins GULPING for air:

NARRATOR (V.O.)

"Oxygen! Oxygen! I need more oxygen! Oh, god - oxygen! OX-Y-GEEEEEN...!"

PERCUSSION ROLL-OUT. Will moves up next to Marko. Last Lock and Attention. Horns come suddenly

MMB

Up!

NARRATOR (V.O.)
At the end of Entry, my lungs were already burning and we hadn't even started yet.

Will PANTS.

NARRATOR (V.O.)
But I was going to play every note Marko did...

Cavendish heaves a downbeat for the "M Fanfare" and Marko DRILLS the 1st Trumpet part - high, loud, and powerful - with Will playing

NARRATOR (V.O.)
...well, okay, about eight octaves lower. But the principle's the same. And somehow...

SAME SCENE - A MINUTE LATER

NARRATOR (V.O.)
...I made it through the opening "Fanfare".

Cavendish CUTS OFF THE LAST NOTE, leaving a single beat for

NARRATOR (V.O.)
Which was the easy part.

before the band LAUNCHES into "The Victors". Entry lines reform and Will takes off downfield.

Locking.

Playing.

Asphyxiating.

NARRATOR (V.O.)
I won't bother trying to explain what it's like during "The Victors". Just... when you're trying The Lock after the movie? Try it again while blowing up an air mattress, okay?

Will's face grows alarmingly crimson.

NARRATOR (V.O.)

Although I had hung in so far, I knew I couldn't keep this up. I wasn't gonna make it. I wasn't gonna be able to play Every Note.

Deep red, Will teeters on the edge of desperation.

NARRATOR (V.O.)

And then it happened.

From the corner of his eye, Will checks on Marko, who takes a breath, then continues steam-rolling alongside him.

Will's eyes go wide:

NARRATOR (V.O.)

Did you see it? Did you see it? I can't believe you didn't see it! Here, run it back, run it back...!

THE FILM REVERSES and Marko repeats his actions:

NARRATOR (V.O.)

<u>There</u>. Did ya...? Okay, here, <u>here</u>...

THE FILM REVERSES A SECOND TIME to the point where Will looks out the corner of his eye:

NARRATOR (V.O.)

Now watch <u>closely</u>...

CLOSE ON - MARKO

IN STYLIZED SLO-MO as he INHALES and EXHALES during the "Hail! Hail!" part of "The Victors":

NARRATOR (V.O.)

Marko took a breath!

As Will's eyes go wide a second time, RESUME NORMAL SPEED:

NARRATOR (V.O.)
He <u>missed</u> two notes! Rested! He just... didn't play 'em! The man with the leather lungs, the thunder thighs - the Premiere Chair of the MMB...

Will now BELTS OUT his 3rd Trumpet part:

NARRATOR (V.O.)
...and I was up on him by two notes! The realization brought me a whole second wind...!

Will quickly relapses to nearly one BREATH per note:

NARRATOR (V.O.)
...which lasted about three seconds. But there was no way I was gonna stop now. I would Lock and Die if necessary, but I was gonna play "Every Note".
(determined)
Through the rest of "The Victors"...

SAME SCENE - A MINUTE LATER

NARRATOR (V.O.)
Through the visiting team's fight song, where the fans *expected* you to miss notes...

SAME SCENE - A MINUTE LATER

NARRATOR (V.O.)
Through the trumpeting "Banner", where I could hear life-giving gasping going on all around me...

SAME SCENE - A MINUTE LATER

NARRATOR (V.O.)
...I played. I played Every Note.

But not without cost. For as horns

MMB

Drop!

at the conclusion of "The Star Spangled Banner" and the CROWD CHEERS, Will is finding that even HYPERVENTILATION can't satisfy his collapsing lungs.

He looks at the sideline:

NARRATOR (V.O.)

Until I could see the finish line just ahead.

TWEET! TWEET! TWEET! TWEET!

MMB

Up!

The Block locks and BEGINS

NARRATOR (V.O.)

One more "Victors". That's all that was left...

Will struggles for the sideline, still playing Every Note:

NARRATOR (V.O.)

I was gonna make it. I was gonna prove to myself that I belonged here, that I deserved this. I was gonna--

BLACKOUT

as the SCREEN GOES COMPLETELY DARK:

NARRATOR (V.O.)

Now, I don't actually remember passing out. What I do remember is...

WILL'S P.O.V. - TWO BLURRED COLORS

SLOWLY FADING INTO VIEW above him:

NARRATOR (V.O.)
...yellow and blue.

VOICES
"Look..." "I think he's coming to..." "His eyes are opening..."

The colors belong to the

PLUMES

of band members bending over him on all sides:

NARRATOR (V.O.)
And a question I still hadn't answered.

PLUME
You all right?

ON THE SIDELINE

Will sits up and looks around him. Nearly the entire Block is gathered, Pregame apparently just concluded.

NARRATOR (V.O.)
There are moments in your life that balance on a knife's edge. That can fall either way. Hero or goat...

Indeed, it seems many of The Block - even the Drum Major and Marko - don't know how to react at this point.

NARRATOR (V.O.)
And sometimes, the nudge that decides it all comes from the highest of powers...

The Block parts and

CAVENDISH

steps in, beatifically severe in his director's uniform. He examines the still seated Will and makes his mighty pronouncement:

CAVENDISH
Now that's giving 150 damn percent!

The band actually SENDS UP A CHEER.

Will quickly finds himself on his feet amidst a flurry of white gloves:

NARRATOR (V.O.)
After that, I became something of a touchstone for the Michigan Marching Band.

The hands continue to PAT and the CROWD takes up the CHEER.

NARRATOR (V.O.)
Sort of a talisman of good luck. From that day forward, my place in The Block was secure.

More and more gather round.

NARRATOR (V.O.)
To have subjected me to another Challenge would have been unthinkable. I had already undergone The Ultimate...

The Trumpet Reserve shakes Will's hand.

NARRATOR (V.O.)
...and won. Even Marko developed a grudging respect.

Along the sideline, where the team itself has turned to APPLAUD, a scowling Marko is encouraged to join in after an elbow from a 300 pound lineman.

To top it all off, Will suddenly finds himself rising on the shoulders of his peers:

NARRATOR (V.O.)
And as I rose into the light of that early September afternoon... and *heard* the support... and *felt* the love... and... <u>and</u>... and you're note really buying any of this, are you?

On the field, Will simply continues to enjoy the ride.

NARRATOR (V.O.)
Come on - the shoulder carry? You really believe that happened?
(facetious)
Oh, uh, by the way, there's a new federal law that just went into effect where everybody who sees this movie has to send five extra bucks to the writer, me, Todd, at 3-1-3 - come on.

People in the stands unfurl a "We (heart) Will!" Banner.

NARRATOR (V.O.)
None of what you're seeing now is true. So why am I showing it?

Photographers begin FLASHING snapshots.

NARRATOR (V.O.)
Because that's the way it should have happened. Everybody should have a moment like that in their life. A movie moment.

POP! Streamers and confetti.

NARRATOR (V.O.)
But the truth is rarely so dramatic. Are you ready for it? Here it is: I never even got challenged until my *second* year in marching band.
(beat)
And I survived.

Media. Cameras. Mikes.

NARRATOR (V.O.)
But that wouldn't have been much of a story. Even though the lessons were just the same.

Cheerleaders.

NARRATOR (V.O.)
And what were those lessons?

Finally, Will bows his head and receives a kiss - and a blue-ribboned medal - from none other than Jeannine Winterspoon.

NARRATOR (V.O.)
What was the point of all this?

CUT TO:

EXT. CAMPUS - DAY

where Will, nicely dressed and carrying a notebook, retraces some of the same steps he took during Freshman Orientation. Only the campus is much more crowded now.

NARRATOR (V.O.)
Well, when I started out, I thought this was going to be just another coming-of-age story. I do a lot of those.

Will strides confidently. He seems a little older.

NARRATOR (V.O.)
You know - transition from high school to college, away from home for the first time - all condensed and intensified by one Hell Week in marching band.

Will spots something of interest.

NARRATOR (V.O.)
In fact, here was the image I was gonna use...

Will steps up to a gawky freshman RATTLING the same glass door that was once locked to Will. He points to the freshman's map and sends him in the right direction.

NARRATOR (V.O.)
Symmetry.

Will continues on his way. A Freshman Veteran.

NARRATOR (V.O.)
But no Closure. What do I mean by "Closure"? Well, here's an example. Not only is it the nearest we're gonna get to a perfect movie moment...

CUT TO:

INT. CLASSROOM - DAY

where Will takes notes:

NARRATOR (V.O.)
...it's also true.

His table is one of many crowded with students.

NARRATOR (V.O.)
We need to skip forward a little to springtime, where I was taking an extra half-term to get ahead in classes. The class itself...

ON THE RAISED STAGE AT THE FRONT OF THE ROOM

where a bespectacled PROFESSOR fills the chalkboard with equations:

NARRATOR (V.O.)
...was Boring As Hell 101. AKA, "Thermodynamics".

PROFESSOR
(droning)

The Second Law states that for all reactions in all systems, open or closed, the entropy - or disorder, "s" - always increases.

NARRATOR (V.O.)
I guess by that time I was sort of an expert in entropy. Because even thought Thermodynamics was taken mostly by seniors who needed a technical elective to graduate...

ON WILL'S NOTE BINDER

where a bluebook with a red-inked "100" protrudes:

NARRATOR (V.O.)
...I had the highest scores in class. I bring this up not to brag - well, okay, that, too - but mostly because...

ON MARKO

a few rows back, struggling to keep up:

NARRATOR (V.O.)
...Marko was also in that class. And Marko...

His pencil SNAPS. He searches for a new one in a panic.

NARRATOR (V.O.)
...needed help.

SAME SCENE - LATER

where Marko stands before Will in the otherwise empty room:

NARRATOR (V.O.)
Which he asked for.

SAME SCENE - LATER

with the positions now reversed - Will standing watch over the scribbling Marko:

NARRATOR (V.O.)

And got.

Will paces in front of the long table where Marko works out a problem.

NARRATOR (V.O.)

Why? Let's just say 5th year seniors were not unknown in the MMB. Besides, there was even a better reason...

Will leans over to check Marko's work.

NARRATOR (V.O.)

Without going into too much detail, calculations of entropy involved a certain step called--

WILL

Did you lock in the variable?

MARKO

Uhhh...

NARRATOR (V.O.)

Come on, Marko, where's the lock? Where's the lock?

Marko gets it. But goes back to work.

NARRATOR (V.O.)

I guess every rule has an exception. Because the entropy in *this* system...

Will resumes his pacing with a grin.

NARRATOR (V.O.)

...provided "Closure".

(beat)

As for the rest of the story...

PRE-LAP

DRUM MAJOR (V.O.)

Everybody up...!

CUT TO:

EXT. ELBERT PRACTICE FIELD - DAY

as The Block springs to attention:

MMB

One!

TWEET! TWEET! TWEET! TWEET!

NARRATOR (V.O.)

...it's time to wrap it all...

MMB

Up!

(beat-beat)

Lock!

The band begins SWEEP DRILL down the field...

...with Will back to his old Rank 8 position between

THOR

Wooooo...! Fire up! It's Monday!

and

CHARLIE

(panting)

Such a shame it would be for Freshman Will to witness your unwelcome pep strangled with my own two bare hands.

Will grins. Even with The Lock, he's beginning to discover that MMB <u>can</u> be fun.

NARRATOR (V.O.)
When I look back on it now, the most amazing thing to me isn't that I survived, but that I got there at all.

Will looks at Reveille Music Hall in the distance.

NARRATOR (V.O.)
That, in fact, is what this story is *really* all about. It's called "The Theme", and in contemporary movie terms is defined as - quote - "that thing we usually don't bother with" - unquote.
(beat)
Well, I'm gonna bother...

Will breaks a sweat, but keeps Locking.

NARRATOR (V.O.)
Any ideas as to what The Theme is? Here, I'll give you a hint...

ON FIGURE #3

marching awkwardly down the field with his trumpet:

NARRATOR (V.O.)
Remember this guy?

CUT TO:

SAME SCENE - A WEEK BEFORE

where Figure #3 amuses The Block:

FIGURE #3
Dupple commaaaaand! A-teeen-shut! A-teeen-shut! One...! Two...! Three...!

NARRATOR (V.O.)
That's right. Drum Major tryouts. Some of you may have even wondered why I spent so much time on this

since it didn't really seem to have anything to do with the story.

ON WILL

trying not to snicker:

NARRATOR (V.O.)
Well, the fact is, it has *everything* to do with the story.

As before, the SNICKER dam bursts.

NARRATOR (V.O.)
I laughed with everyone else at this guy. And for the longest time, I thought of him as just some tragic loser.

Figure #3 holds his baton at marbleized attention.

NARRATOR (V.O.)
But I know different now. I didn't realize it until years later - when I started writing this movie - but what this kid did is *exactly* what I learned from my marching band experience.

Figure #3 hasn't blinked, even amidst the SNICKERING.

NARRATOR (V.O.)
It has to do with doing things you're scared to do. Doing things when the odds are against you. Doing things that everyone else thinks you shouldn't.

Will finally begins to note the implacability of the Figure standing before him.

NARRATOR (V.O.)
It has to do with The Theme of this movie and here it is:

RESUME - SWEEP DRILL

with Will sweating even more, but still Locking:

NARRATOR (V.O.)
"The greatest tragedy isn't trying and failing, but never trying at all."

The Sweep continues, no end in sight.

NARRATOR (V.O.)
Too simple? Too obvious? Too bad. Because that's what it is. It took me a long, long time to learn it - and I'll bet there are one or two of you out there who could still benefit from the lesson.

Lock, lock, lock.

NARRATOR (V.O.)
Now, usually, you're not supposed to just outright state The Theme of a movie. It's too blunt. It's bad form. It's just not done.

INSERT TITLE CARD:

"Theme: The greatest tragedy isn't trying and failing, but never trying at all."

RESUME

on Will:

NARRATOR (V.O.)
That's The Theme of "My Marching Band Story".

Lock, lock, lock.

NARRATOR (V.O.)
It's how I became a member of one of the best bands in the country.

Lock, lock.

NARRATOR (V.O.)
It's how I stayed a member of one of the best bands in the country.

Lock.

NARRATOR (V.O.)
And...

FREEZE FRAME

NARRATOR (V.O.)
...it's how I made a movie about being a member of one of the best bands in the country.

The Block SLOWLY DISSOLVES from the field.

NARRATOR (V.O.)
Because, for me personally - Me, The Storyteller now - that's what this has really been all about.

The LIGHT on the field BEGINS TO FADE.

NARRATOR (V.O.)
After graduating from college, I didn't stay an engineer for long. I started writing scripts. And eventually, I even started selling scripts. But it wasn't enough.

DARKNESS has now descended on the field.

NARRATOR (V.O.)
I wanted to make what I wrote. But I was scared. I kept waiting for other people to give me the opportunity, instead of going out and trying to make a movie on my own. Directing...

FIELD LIGHTS POP ON, illuminating

A FLUTTERING FLAG

at midfield:

NARRATOR (V.O.)
...had become my new Jeannie Winterspoon.

The flag DISSOLVES away, leaving

EXT. ELBERT PRACTICE FIELD - NIGHT

empty once again...

...except for a lone FIGURE now standing at its center:

NARRATOR (V.O.)
Until now.

VERY HIGH ANGLE - CRANING DOWN

toward the Figure:

NARRATOR (V.O.)
I don't know how it came out. That'll be up to you to decide. But I do know this:

THE SHOT COMES CLOSER, the Figure wearing a band jacket:

NARRATOR (V.O.)
"The greatest tragedy isn't trying and failing, but never trying at all."

THE SAME SHOT settles on the sleeve of the jacket and a patch that reads "Super Bowl".

IT CONTINUES UP past other bowl patches: Astro Blue-Bonnet, Gator, and Rose:

NARRATOR (V.O.)
If that's too much to remember, let me sum it up for you in just one word.

THE SHOT NOW TRACKS across the shoulder, catching some embroidery on the chest: "Todd", and below, "Trumpet".

NARRATOR (V.O.)

The next time you're thinking of doing or not doing something you'd really like to do...

THE SHOT FINALLY SETTLES on the face, where a hint of a grin advises

TODD

"March."

And with "My Marching Band Story" thus coming down to just one word

CUT TO:

BLACK

and a by now familiar

TWEET! TWEET! TWEET! TWEET!

followed by FOUR SHARP SNARE BEATS and

INT. MICHIGAN STADIUM - DAY

FROM HIGH UP IN THE STANDS as

THE MMB

BURSTS onto the field from the tunnel

and

THE FINAL CREDITS ROLL.

This is the first time the band's signature Pregame will be seen the way it was meant to be seen, from above...

...though the tiny figures below may somehow seem even closer than before:

ENTRY

FOLD-OUT TO SOLID BLOCK "M"

THE "M Fanfare", TRUMPETS BLAZING

ENTRY LINES REFORMED

"The Victors" DOWN THE FIELD

HOLLOW BLOCK "M" BACK UP THE FIELD

But instead of what traditionally follows, the band scatters in double-time

ENTRY CADENCE

to another formation where they SCREAM and mark time until

THE FINAL LOCK

thunders to earth and

PLUMED HATS

ascend into the Blue and

FREEZE FRAME

on the last words written:

Not

FADE OUT:

but

"THE END"

All About Todd

1960: Born.

1961-1982: Grew up. Did non-writing stuff.

1983-1985: Worked with NASA as Aerospace Engineer. Started writing scripts part-time for no money.

1986-1987: Started writing scripts full-time for no money.

1988-1990: Wrote for first two seasons of "THE WONDER YEARS". Nominated for Emmy, Humanitas, and Writers Guild Awards. Won Humanitas and Writers Guild. Lost Emmy to pilot of "Murphy Brown" but I'm not bitter anymore especially since show never lived up to its potential.

Wrote the first two "TEENAGE MUTANT NINJA TURTLES" movies. Became rich, but with occasional pangs of guilt.

1991-1992: Tried to elevate the quality of films coming out of Holywood by rejecting all script assignments and writing only on spec. I.E., Obscurity and Unemployment.

1993-1995: Ran away to Europe for a few months, returned, wrote first play. Ran away to Asia for a few months, returned, directed first short film.

1996: Stopped running long enough to get in line to write a feature film version of "I Dream of Jeannie". BLINK! Next.

1997-1999: Completed Quest for Seven Continents with travels to Africa, Australia, South America, and Antarctica (whiter even than The Blank Page).

2000-2002: Solidified reputation as International Man of Leisure. Blew it by writing a book in here somewhere.

2003-2005: Nap.

2006-2007: Wrote, produced, and directed a 90-minute compilation of comedy shorts called "42 STORY HOUSE". Sold very nearly that many DVD'S.

2008-2009: Pangs of guilt concerning sudden wealth now a distant memory, sought status as "Too Big To Fail". Failed.

2010: Attempted to finance an indie movie called "WHY THE SQUIRREL WON'T FRY". Fried.

2011: Published first eBook "THE TELLING OF MY MARCHING BAND STORY". Achieved Complete World Domination. (Pending)

www.ToddTrumpet.com

Made in the USA
San Bernardino, CA
03 September 2015